A Caprice
Romance

THREE'S A CROWD

NOLA CARLSON

ACE TEMPO BOOKS, NEW YORK

THREE'S A CROWD
A Caprice Romance
Copyright © 1982 by Nola Carlson

An Ace Tempo Book

ISBN: 0-448-16921-5

First Ace Tempo Edition: August 1982
Second Printing: October 1982

Tempo Books is registered in the United States Patent Office

Published simultaneously in Canada

Manufactured in the United States of America

Ace Books, 200 Madison Avenue, New York, New York 10016

Chapter 1

Karen propped her chin on the spiral notebook that was in her lap. Squinting into the sun, she tried to focus on Marc Rodgers who sprinted across the track at the opposite side of the field. A tremble, like a cold chill, raced through her body. As she concentrated on his effortless, graceful strides with head reared back and chest thrust forward Marc reminded her of a handsome thoroughbred. He was sleek, not an ounce of excess fat on his body, with muscles that rippled beneath taut skin. Each stride was geared to extract the maximum distance —springing up on his toes, landing on the balls of his feet. A shock of jet black hair blew back from his forehead as he came around the last turn reaching the finish line far ahead of his nearest competitor.

Karen was amazed that even after the wrenchingly exhausting 1,500 meter he was hardly out of breath merely walking, head down, for a time his hands placed on his narrow hips. Marc Rodgers was an Adonis compared to the other boys at Central High, she thought. She had

1

assessed that the first time she saw him and would always remember that day.

Karen had been in the student cafeteria line and had her tray poked forward to receive her lunch when he walked by. She remembered accidentally moving the tray as she did a double take to notice Marc. She recalled his easy, relaxed gait and the slight, confident tilt of his head. Craning her neck to get the very last glimpse possible of his broad shoulders, she watched him exit through the cafeteria doors. It was an exit any Hollywood actor would have been proud of. With a sigh, she turned to look back up at the disgruntled cook who had spooned Karen's lunch onto the counter then, in a sarcastic tone, asked her whether she was ready to be served.

Since that day in the cafeteria, Karen had "bird-dogged" Marc Rodgers to the point of absurdity. From the school office, she had wheedled her friend Margie to reveal his classification, age, and address. Margie had protested at first arguing that it was against school policy to make such information accessible. But when Karen promised to loan her the salmon-colored skirt she was so fond of for the spring K-ette tea Margie gave in. Karen stood watch at Dr. Melford's door while Margie's fingers flew through the R's to extricate the information from the file.

Karen's mind had spun in a pink whirlwind as she skipped down the concrete steps of Central High that day. "Marc Rodgers," she rolled the name over her tongue several times accentuating one syllable and then another. Quickly, she concluded, that anyway you said it, it was beautiful, it was poetry. She was only able to get his vital statistics—he was eighteen years old, a senior, and his address was 1804 Dartmouth Drive—before Dr. Melford stepped through the office door, his gray, bushy brows furrowed, his perpetual scowl intact.

Margie's face had visibly blanched as she whirled back to the filing cabinet to replace the card. Karen had abruptly changed the conversation to acquiring information as to whether she had any late notices thus far on her record this current quarter. Dr. Melford, called the Fox by students and a few cautious faculty members for his astute summation of dubious situations, had stood frowning until Karen left. The old principal had been in the school system for thirty years as a teacher, counselor, vice principal, and principal and could, by this time, "smell out" a situation that appeared to be suspect. He, at times, had entered classrooms unannounced on the premonition that something was not quite right. More often than not, he was needed at that particular moment.

Immediately, after cheerleading practice that day, Karen drove her 1969 orange VW, dubbed the Pumpkin, to the northeast section of town searching out 1804 Dartmouth Drive. She found the house to be a comfortable split level with a neatly shorn lawn and a two-foot hedge circumventing its border. A 1979 maroon Camaro, with a jacked-up rearend, had been carefully backed into the drive. The sun reflected off of a surrealistic design of a spider on the hood. Karen thought it was a dream wagon of all time. For just a moment, she eased The Pumpkin to the opposite curb and stared at the residence of her Adonis. Consciously, she realized that she was acting like a moonstruck calf, but no one in her sixteen years had affected her in this way.

Since that first day, she had driven past his house countless times, waited for him at the Pit (a favorite high school hangout), watched him walk by in the halls, stand in line in the cafeteria, and mused over him at track practice. She was becoming more and more convinced that she wouldn't draw his notice even if she grew an extra head.

"Still star gazin', Karen?"

Karen looked up to see Sandy slide in beside her on the bleachers. As usual, her glasses set precipitously on the tip of her nose looking as if the slightest jar would send them toppling off. Sandy's eyes were magnified beneath the thick lenses.

Karen tossed a stray strand of auburn hair back with a jolt of her head, a familiar habit. Even out in the strong wind, her hair in disarray, she looked pretty. Many girls envied her startling good looks. It disgusted some how easily attainable it was for her. She had inherited her high, prominent cheek bones, flawless complexion, and patrician nose from her mother who had been a beauty in her own right in her younger days. Upon the first warm days of summer her skin tanned a coppery color avoiding the peeling redness of sunburn which plagued others. Karen didn't have to go through the time-consuming, tedious beauty rituals of other girls. She had been blessed with thick, lustrous hair that cascaded naturally to her shoulders in subtle waves. With a dab of lip gloss and a swoop of a mascara brush she was ready for anything. An overused expression, "natural good looks," certainly applied in her case.

Karen smiled but continued to look toward the track as she nudged her best friend with her elbow. "I might as well be one of the starting blocks for all he cares."

Sandy sighed allowing her breath to sift through her slightly protuberant teeth. "He is quite a man, I'll agree. He would be a prize for any girl." She glanced over to Karen. "If anyone has a chance with him, you do."

Karen shrugged, contorting her face. "Oh, sure. I've done everything but lie down in his path and I'm about ready to try that next."

"Well, at least he'd have to step on you or over you. He couldn't help but notice," Sandy said giggling.

Sandy's laugh was infectious, as always, and Karen found herself bursting into giggles as well. The two of them had been close friends ever since Junior High. Sandy's parents moved to Riverview four years ago when her father was transferred. Karen liked Sandy's warmth and humor immediately. She always had an ear willing to listen and a shoulder ready to comfort. Sandy, Karen thought, was like a port in a storm—always there when it was needed. The two of them had been almost inseparable until lately. Karen had been casually dating for over a year and up to now, Sandy had never been asked out. She sat on the risers among the wallflowers in the gym praying for some boy to ask her to dance. Once in a while, when the prospects seemed hopeless, she would grab another girl and they would dance pretending to have fun. Karen knew how she was hurting inside. She physically ached for her friend, at these times, sure that if some boy would take the time and interest to develop a relationship with her he would see what a special person she was.

Abruptly, Sandy covered her eyes, peeking through her fingers. "Don't look now, Karen, but he's looking this way."

Karen's heart started to pound.

"He's walking over here!" Sandy squealed clutching her breast. "I think I'm going to die!"

"Act natural," Karen admonished. "Just act natural. We don't want to scare him off." Self-consciously, she pulled at her sweater, brushed at the wrinkles in her skirt and smoothed her hair. Admittedly, she was embarrassed at her reaction as he neared.

"The closer he gets the better he gets," Sandy whispered shifting about on her wooden seat. "He must be way over six feet tall."

Karen nudged her friend in the ribs once again.

"And that black hair! Did you ever see such black hair? I swear, it's black as pitch!"

"Will you be quiet! He's almost here," Karen whispered from the corner of her mouth.

"I've got chills all over my arms. Look, Karen, at all of those goose bumps."

Karen swiped Sandy's arm away dropping her notebook. As she bent to pick it up her eyes settled on a pair of track shoes standing before her. She followed up the tanned, muscular legs, narrow hips, broad chest, and looked into the deepest blue eyes she had ever seen shrouded with thick, dark lashes. A cleft indented his strong, squared chin. Karen's breath caught as she reared back against her seat clutching the notebook to her chest.

"Either of you girls have the time?" His voice came out deep and resonant disguising his youth.

Karen's mouth remained agape as she struggled to speak. Sandy sat frozen as though she had suddenly become mummified.

Mechanically, Karen thrust her arm forward presenting her wrist. The boy leaned forward, lightly grasping her wrist, and read the time.

"Five fifteen. Thanks a lot." He turned and jogged off calling back over his shoulder, "See ya."

For several moments both girls sat immobile and mute as they watched him return to the track readying himself for a 440 relay.

Finally, Karen moaned and beat her notebook against the side of her head. "Oh, what a klutz! If he never looks at me again I won't be surprised. He probably thinks I can't even tell time."

Sandy sat limp, the color gradually returning to her livid face. "Oh, he can't be real! No one is that gorgeous." She turned to Karen. "Did you hear that voice? I've never heard a voice that deep coming from a high school guy." Closing her eyes, she rubbed her forehead. "I'll bet he's been shaving for three years!"

Karen turned and looked into the thick glasses. "That's real heavy, Sandy. The point is, here I am trailing him like a bloodhound for weeks and when he finally does come up to me I can't even speak." She slumped down into her seat. "I wish I were dead."

Sandy encircled her friend's shoulder and gave her a bolstering hug. "Forget it. Maybe he's not worth all of this agony."

"Not worth it?" Karen gasped in disbelief. "He's just the best thing that's ever happened to Central High in the last decade, that's all. I can't study, eat, or sleep since I saw him that day in the cafeteria." Holding her arms out straight, she gestured. "I'm a walking zombie. My mom and dad think my brains have gone into early hibernation."

Sandy rolled her eyes in apology. "Forget I said that. He is worth all the agony."

Karen shook her head as though she were trying to clear her mind. "Let's get out of here. This is torture. I feel like a kid in a candy store without a penny to her name."

Sandy whistled. "Boy, you *have* got it bad."

Karen cradled her notebook in her arms as she walked toward the school parking lot. "I know it's crazy." She made an effort to rationalize her feelings. "I've had crushes before." Turning her head, she grinned sheepishly. "Remember that infatuation I had on our gym teacher, Mr. Briar, in the ninth grade?" She sighed. "What a dream. Big muscles, broad shoulders, the whole bit."

"Yeah," Sandy acknowledged, "but it turned into a nightmare when you found out he had a wife and five kids."

Karen muffled her mouth as she giggled.

Throwing her head back, Sandy joined the hilarity. "Yeah, we were going to send him anonymous love notes and slip them into his locker. We even thought about calling his wife to see if she really needed him."

They supported one another growing weak from laughter.

Wiping the tears from her eyes with one hand and rubbing her aching ribs with the other, Sandy sighed. "We were such kids then."

Karen playfully boxed her on the shoulder. "Yes, that was all of three years ago."

"Well, since then, you know better than to reach for the moon."

"What do you think I'm doing now? I might as well be in love with Robert Redford."

"There's always Spike," Sandy offered casually. "He's been in the wings waiting for you for years."

A thoughtful crease deepened on Karen's forehead. "Yeah, Spike's great. He's kind, faithful, and always in a good mood."

"The only thing you left out is obedient and you'd be describing your pet Cocker Spaniel, Karen."

Karen tossed a tendril of hair back over her shoulders with a flip of her fingers. "Oh, you know

I don't mean it that way. It's just that he's more of a . . ." She thought for a moment. 'A buddy." Turning, she hoped she had convinced her friend. "Spike and I have grown up together. My folks and his have been friends ever since we were little kids. The two of us used to play in our backyard when we were little, swinging on the jungle gym and splashing each other in my plastic wading pool. I even used to help him deliver papers and played right field on his baseball team. He's a real special friend." She emphasized the word "friend."

"I think he's neat."

"Spike *is* a great guy. Some girl would be lucky to catch him."

"You know he doesn't want anybody but you don't you, Karen?"

Turning her head abruptly, a doubtful expression emerged on Karen's face.

"On, come on. You can't be that blind. He's been crazy about you for years."

"Yes, as a friend. Spike dates two or three girls."

Sandy bandied her head about, her glasses sliding further down her nose. "No, not just as a friend. And I don't care if he dates a dozen or more girls."

"Ah, Sandy, you've read one too many romance magazines." Pausing, she waved her notebook about in a melodramatic gesture. "The boy with the secret longing for the girl next door. Years pass as they play together as children, scuffling about, making mudpies and sand castles, competing on the same little league, etcetera, etcetera." She pointed her finger to the sky. "And then one day they accidentally touch while studying for an American History test. Eyes meet, pulses race, and they both know that they've been in love all along." Karen threw her head back and laughed disappointedly noticing that her friend failed to join her this time.

Sandy shrugged in reconciliation. "What's the old adage about not being able to see the forest for the trees? Laugh if you want to but I, as an outsider, see things that you're not even aware of, Karen Marie Cooper. I see the way he looks at you and hangs on to your every word. I see how hurt he is when you drive off with another guy." She looked down at the ground morosely. "I should be so lucky." She tapped on the lens of her thick glasses. "I can see, girl. I can see."

Karen mused silently as she chewed on her inner lip. "Spike is more like a . . . a brother. I could never think of him in any other way."

"All I can say, he sure doesn't think of you as a sister."

Karen was prepared for a rebuttal until her eye caught the sight of Marc Rodger's maroon Camaro sitting in the lot only a few cars down from the Pumpkin. She advanced slowly toward it as though she were looking at a vision, running her fingers delicately over its gleaming, chrome grill. "Isn't this something, Sandy? You wouldn't even have to see the owner to know he's neat with a car like this."

"Oh, I don't know," Sandy shrugged, "I've seen some real duds climb out of neat cars."

"Don't be so negative!" Karen reprimanded.

"Sorry." Sandy nodded her head. "I've got to admit in this case the car does match its owner."

Suddenly a stark expression coated Karen's face. Her eyes glazed and a flush slowly crept up her throat. "I couldn't." She shook her head emphatically. "No, I just couldn't. That would be going too far. After all, I've never been forward with a guy in my life. My policy has always been to be the pursued not the pursuer." A finger accentuated her decision on the edge of her notebook.

Sandy stood there listening to the monologue a quizzical expression on her face. "Could I get in on this conversation or is this just between you and yourself?"

Karen emerged from her revery reluctantly. "Sorry, kid. I was just debating with myself."

Sandy placed her hands on her full, slightly rotund waist. "That much was obvious."

Walking furtively toward Sandy, Karen glanced over her shoulder. Leaning forward, she spoke in a hushed voice. "Well, here I am not five feet from his car."

"That much is also obvious."

"I thought maybe I could drop a note in the seat." She continued to explain. "You know something casual, friendly." She placed a finger on Sandy's lips. "Don't answer until you've thought about it."

Sucking on her front teeth, Sandy thought to herself. At last, she nodded. "Like what?"

"Oh, I don't know," Karen said impatiently.

"Help me out; you're my best friend."

"Okay, give me space." She moved her arms about in a wide arc and Karen stepped back. Rolling her eyes back into her head Sandy chewed on the tip of her pencil in reflection.

Karen watched her anxiously, fully realizing that her friend was far more competent in composition than she. It was as though a sign should be posted stating: Quiet! Genius at Work!

Poking her glasses back up on her nose, she tapped the pencil lead against her lower teeth as she thought. Once her eyes widened and Karen lurched forward only to see her shake her head dismissing the idea. Again she submerged herself into creative thinking. Suddenly, she pursed her lips and nodded in self-agreement. "How's this? 'Have admired you from afar. Would like a chance to get to know you better. If you are the slightest bit interested call 915-6773.'"

Karen winced. "Might be a slight bit forward, don't you think?"

A frown pulled at the corners of Sandy's mouth.

"No. No, it's good," Karen said hurriedly trying to appease her. "I just thought maybe it could be less . . . less pushy."

"Dropping a note in a guy's car is pushy, Karen. What do you want from me?" Sandy huffed, a bit miffed.

Karen nodded her commitment. "Okay, let's use it." Glancing back over her shoulder stealthily, she tore a sheet of paper from her notebook and scrawled out the message. Her lips moved decisively as she checked it over after she finished. "I want to be sure there're no misspelled words. That's all I need for him to be sure I'm a dummy after that wristwatch business." Carefully, she folded it. "Watch for anyone while I slip this in the window of his car."

"I love this!" Sandy exclaimed with excitement. "It's just like James Bond!"

Karen watched the folded paper careen about in the air finally landing conspicuously on the seat. Looking back with a sly smile, she brushed her hands together. "Mission accomplished. Come on, let's move. I'll give you a lift home in the Pumpkin."

Chapter 2

Karen tossed her notebook down on the divan in the living room and charged toward the kitchen. Her appetite was ravenous as she searched through the plastic containers in the refrigerator for food to concoct a sandwich. Her sandwiches, she acknowledged, were culinary works of art. Another one of Karen's blessings was that she could eat endlessly never adding a pound to her weight. Not once had she deviated above one hundred ten since junior high. Calories seemed to burn up instantly due to her endless activity. She was class officer, student council member, cheerleader, and managed to maintain a solid B average each quarter. Her mother always said, even when she slept she was in motion, as the muddle of twisted covers would attest to in the morning.

Karen was interested in every facet of life, involving herself completely in her school and home life. She felt sorry for the girls who complained about their families. She felt that her family was extraordinary in its closeness. Much of this, she attributed to Dody, her younger sister who was born with Down's Syndrome. Ever since Dody was born she had been a catalyst that pulled the family together.

Mrs. Cooper had explained, four months after Dody's birth, that she was a Down's Syndrome child, better known as mongoloid, and in all probability, would never attain the mental capacity beyond the age of six.

At first, the family had lapsed into a futile sadness and regret asking themselves why such a thing had happened to them. But once they met and talked with other people who had Mongoloid children they began to look forward to raising and loving Dody. They were not disappointed. She had been a joy throughout her ten years. She was uninhibited and expressed her love openly and often. If she liked someone, even a stranger, she professed it with a warm hug and an offer of friendship. This openess startled and even repelled some people. Even if they showed distaste, Dody was innocently unaware of how they felt continuing to like them just as much. As she became older, her eyes acquired the characteristic oriental slant and her reddish hair grew in fine and sparse. A facial expression she used frequently was grimacing as though she suddenly had tasted something bitter. Some people misunderstood this expression. They all had to be quite cautious with Dody's health as Down's Syndrome children were highly susceptible to colds and frequently had bad hearts. Dody attended a TMR (Trainable Mentally Retarded) class in a public school and was making remarkable progress even though she was far behind her chronological age.

Balancing a glass of milk, apple, sandwich, and a teen magazine in her arms, Karen made the precipitous trek back to the living room managing not to spill a drop. Depositing her lunch on the glass top of the coffee table, she sighed as she sank deeply into the velour cushions. With a toe of one shoe she dug at the heel of the other pushing it off and then reversing the order. Tucking her feet beneath her, Karen bit into the apple with a crunch that sounded explosive in the silent house. Carelessly, she flipped through the pages without interest seeing the pictures but failing to have the mental images register in her brain. Usually, she looked forward to each issue of *Teen Talk* examining each page closely, absorbing current trends in clothing and hair styles. Today was different. The pictures flew by in a bright collage with little notice as her mind wandered back to Marc Rodgers. Would he find the note and if he did would he call? If he did call would he ask her out? Perhaps, he would just laugh at it as though it were a joke. A tremble of dread shook her body.

A frown settled on her face at the thought that he might think she was terribly forward and automatically cross her off his list. Pushy girls could be real turn-offs, she had heard some guys say. But, if she did wait for him to make a move it might never happen. A relationship might never develop.

Karen slapped at her forehead with the flat of

her hand in disgust. What was happening to her? She was acting like a thirteen-year-old kid who had never had a date. Suppose this guy wasn't interested in her? It certainly wouldn't be the end of the world. What was this weird obsession she had about him, anyway? There were plenty of cute, nice boys at Central High. Why get all strung out over one guy? There was even Spike if no one else was available. Suddenly, her appetite evaporated and she threw down the half-eaten apple and looked vacantly above the magazine. What a horrible thing to think; she bit into her lower lip sullenly.

Abruptly, she was jolted from her thoughts by the slamming of the front door and a tumultuous warhoop. Karen looked up to see Dody running toward her, her tightly woven red braids flying. She was grinning from ear to ear, her arms extended. Karen cherished the diversion and moved forward to receive her in an embrace. Dody screamed as she soared over the coffee table into her sister's arms. The glass of milk toppled over, spilling its contents out onto the beige shag rug. For a moment no one was aware of it as Dody hugged and kissed her.

"Dody, look what you've done! You go right into the kitchen and get something to wipe up that mess at once!" Mrs. Cooper admonished.

Dody cringed at the sound of her mother's brittle voice and looked back. She winced as she looked down at the puddle of milk on the coffee table and the damp spot on the rug. "I sorry mama."

Mrs. Cooper sighed patiently. "That's all right,

Dody, but you must be more careful. I've told you about running in the house." Her brows arched. "Don't you remember that?"

Dody smiled, having an instant revelation. "I remember that, mama."

Mrs. Cooper smiled. "Good. Now, go on and get a towel to wipe up the milk."

Dody bounded from Karen's arms, racing for the kitchen, already forgetting the instructions about not running in the house.

Mrs. Cooper smiled shaking her head with acquiescence. Finally, her attention was drawn to her elder daughter. "How was your day, dear?"

"Fine, mom," Karen answered distractedly.

"You don't sound too enthused."

Karen, determined not to allow her mother to know about her interest in the new boy, smiled and made an attempt to appear effervescent. "It was good! We learned a couple of neat routines this afternoon. Thought we might use them at the opening football game next year."

"Anything else?"

Karen looked down playing with the hem of her skirt unable to look into her mother's eyes. Karen had always known she had the unique gift of not only looking at someone but straight through them when she thought something was troubling them. "No. Same old thing. Got a test in Government Monday. I just knew old Price would throw that on us over the weekend."

"At least you'll have time to study for it." Her attention was diverted for a moment as she saw

Dody reurning with a new dish towel. She looked so pleased that Mrs. Cooper did not have the heart to send her back for an older one.

"I wipe it with this," Dody exclaimed proudly waving the towel about.

"That would be fine, dear."

Peering closely at the table, Dody swiped at the spilled milk diligently. Mrs. Cooper sat watching her allowing her to take responsibility for her own actions. Mustn't overprotect her, she mentally reminded herself. Many a time she bit into her lip to keep from lurching forward to do the task herself. Each time she cautioned herself as she mentally heard Dody's teacher's words echoing in her brain. "Let Dody do as much as she can possibly do. Don't baby or coddle her. If you expect a lot from her she will reward you with a lot. Expect little and she will give little in return."

With mechanical, precise movements she worked at the spill until it was entirely obliterated. Grinning, she turned around in triumph. "I done, mama."

"It looks very good, Dody." Again the words echoed on the importance of praise. "Now, you will be careful won't you, next time?"

Dody bobbed her head up and down in exaggerated affirmation sinking down beside Karen on the couch. Looking up at her sister, she grimaced. "You smell good, Karen. I like the way you smell." Dody always told it exactly the way it was; there was never anything devious or pretentious about her.

Nuzzling her sister's cheek, Karen nipped playfully at her short, rust-colored braids. "So do you, Punkin'." Surreptitiously, Karen dug at her ribs sending her, at once, into giggling hysterics. Dody, laughing out of control, reached out seeking to tickle her older sister in return. Feigning to be off balance, Karen screamed pulling Dody from the divan atop her. The two of them rolled about on the rug giggling and screaming.

Dody had always been good for Karen when she felt lonely or depressed. She had so much against her with the multiple handicaps of retardation and fragile health. Yet, she was always happy, always loving. At times, Karen felt overcome with guilt when she started to indulge in self-pity for she realized that compared to Dody, she had everything. Everything had always come comparatively easy for her. She was pretty and popular with a quick, alert mind. Life had been so kind to her. She caught herself wondering, many times, why she was given everything and Dody so little. And then, she would look into Dody's innocent, sparkling green eyes and know that she was one of the most happy, contented people she had ever encountered. Simple pleasures thrilled her. Dody was friendly and uninhibited, exhibiting a perfect love in a smug, imperfect world. Years ago, Karen would smoulder with rage when she and Dody would go on one of their frequent trips to the park and someone, unintentionally or otherwise, made remarks debasing or pitying her. For a time, Karen would counter with caustic remarks. As the years wore on she saw that the one it bothered least of all was Dody and she was able to control herself. Dody was always there brimming with love whether the person was friend or foe. For those who backed away, repelled or embarrassed, Karen realized that it was their hangup and she felt sorry for them.

Mrs. Cooper deciphered the metallic clang of the doorbell beneath the shrill din of the girls' laughter and hurried to answer it.

Karen giggled as she sparred playfully with Dody. Crossing her eyes, draping her tongue out of the corner of her mouth, she groaned toppling backwards on the rug lying KO'd for the full count. Tears of mirth streamed down Dody's flushed face as she looked down at her sister.

". . . six, seven, eight, nine, ten! The winna'!" Spike Marshall grabbed Dody's arm and hoisted it into the air in a gesture of victory.

Karen continued to lie on the floor pretending to hear bells. Abruptly, she would sit upright cupping her ears only to fall back into a heap calling out for the bells to stop ringing.

Spike positioned his fist beneath Dody's lips pantomiming a microphone. He leaned down intent on the interview. "Anything to say to our boxing fans out there in TV land, champ?"

Dody looked up and grimaced not knowing quite how to respond even though she realized it was all in fun.

"Don't be modest, Champ, tell us where you learned that terrific uppercut." Spike paused rolling his eyes with interest as though she were filling him in on the facts. "I see. Mohammed Ali, you say." He patted her on the back. "You've been taught by the best." With a look of interest he pushed up the sleeve of her T-shirt and felt the slight protuberance of her bicep. "Hard as a rock, Champ. You must really work out."

Dody stood rigid, her arm doubled, a quizzical smile on her lips, not quite understanding, but thoroughly enjoying every moment of it.

"Can you reveal your next opponent, Champ?" He nudged Karen with the toe of his sneaker. "I mean, after easily defeating this dud, you may find the next one a bit more formidable."

Karen looked up frowning. "Ask him who he thinks he is, Howard Cosell, with those multi-syllable words?"

"Tell her, that I'm a better Howard Cosell than she is a boxer any day," Spike countered.

"Tell this Turkey to get off the air or he'll find himself lying flat on his back on the canvas."

"Ask this kultz she and who else would do it?"

Dody's head bandied from one to the other, a look of distress on her face, tears welling in her eyes. "Are you mad?" She shook her head. "I don't want you and Karen to be mad."

Before either of them could explain, she pulled Karen's hand up and placed it in Spike's.

Karen struggled to answer. "Punkin'. . . honey, you don't understand. Spike and I are just kidding."

Spike looked down at his large hand enfolding Karen's and blushed, his mottled, freckled face turning crimson. Abruptly, as though he had just experienced an electric shock, he pulled it free and rubbed it along the smooth, worn material of his old jeans.

Karen placed her hand behind her back.

Recovering his composure quickly, Spike started to playfully punch Dody in the stomach. Her fright at once evaporated as ripples of giggles poured from her grinning mouth.

Grateful for the distraction and even more thankful that her "all-seeing, all-knowing" mother had gone to the kitchen, Karen jumped to her feet and started to take the dishes from the coffee table. Her forehead involuntarily creased as she thought about the strange reaction he had had holding her hand only moments ago. Sounds of giggles and rough-housing bordered her thoughts in the background. Perhaps, it was just one of those rare moments when she and Spike were serious. Karen shrugged. That had to be it. There was no other explanation. A smile emerged on her face. The two of them had been pals since they were children. Sandy's unwelcomed voice pushed into the foreground of her thoughts. "You can't be that blind. He's been crazy about you for years." Glancing quizzically over her shoulder, she viewed the big, lumbersome red-haired boy rolling about the floor trying to escape the flailing fists of the little retarded girl. His arms and face were covered with hordes of freckles appearing that he had been splattered with red paint. Karen suddenly realized, that in all of these years, she had never really looked at Spike. If someone were to ask what he looked like she would have to give them a general, sketchy description. She rationalized: people who were always there like comfortable, old over-stuffed chairs and taken for granted were not thought of in any particular way. They seemed to conjure no emotion. Sometimes, she suddenly realized, she never even thought of him as a separate entity. He was and always had been good old Spike, the best friend a person could ever have.

As Dody fell upon his chest pinning him to the floor, he looked up catching Karen looking back with a serious, thoughtful expression on her face. He smiled up to her and rolled over taking Dody with him.

Spike's uncontrolled voice erupted in oral spasmodic jerks as he continued to wrestle with Dody. "Want . . . to study government . . . Karen?" His voice caught as Dody started tickling him under the arms and his words were inter-mingled with high-pitched giggles. "That test . . . of old Price's is probably . . . going . . . to be a . . . bear."

"Sure, why not? Might as well get it over with so that it doesn't ruin the whole weekend."

He groaned. "Let me capture this little monkey and put her in her cage and we can get to it," he said, easily pinioning Dody to the floor. Her pitiful struggles were easily overcome as she called out her surrender.

Karen smiled, nodding her head. She enjoyed watching the two of them. The hall phone rang, interrupting her thoughts. Mrs. Cooper called out from the kitchen.

"Get that, please, Karen. And send Dody in here; I want her to set the table."

Lying on her back on the rug, Dody wrinkled her nose in distaste.

"Okay, mom," Karen called back. She pointed down to her sister. "You heard mom . . . march!" Turning, Karen briskly walked to the hall as the phone continued to ring. "Hello?" Instantly, a chill reverberated through her body as a deep, familiar voice spoke on the other end. It was the voice she had heard briefly less than two hours ago.

"Is this 915-6773?"

Karen attempted to swallow feeling her throat constrict. "Yes . . . yes." She winced realizing her voice sounded strange, anemic. Clearing her throat, she made an effort to sound more at ease. "Yes, it is."

The voice hesitated as she heard a rustling of paper being unfolded. Karen stood there watching her hand shake as she held the receiver. Abruptly, she placed the receiver in her other hand.

"Well, I found this note in the seat of my car about an hour ago." He started to read. 'Have admired you from afar. Would like a chance to get to know you better. If you are the slightest bit interested call . . . well, you know your own phone number."

Perfunctorily, Karen followed along as he read the note visibly cringing with embarrassment. Now the contents sounded so corny, so juvenile. "Yes

26

. . . yes, I do." She winced and bit into her lip. She knew that by now he must think she was a bumbling idiot.

"Well?" he paused.

"Well?" she replied.

"Well, are you the admirer?" He said it so forceful, so direct, that she was taken off-guard for a moment.

"I . . . I suppose I am. I mean, yes, I am." Sighing, she slapped her forehead with frustration noticing its dampness. From the kitchen she could hear her mother, Dody, and Spike talking and laughing. "Listen," she tried to sound at ease. "I'm really sorry. I've never done anything like this before in my life." Pausing, she expected him to reply but he waited for her to explain further. Karen could never remember being in such mortal agony. Sweat ran down her face in tiny riverlets and her mouth was so dry she couldn't swallow. Why, she thought, did it feel so much like an interrogation? "I mean, it was really a childish thing to do. I really should have known better."

"Then, it's not true?" His voice sounded calm and confident.

Karen dug at the flesh in her inner cheek. Girls must chase him all of the time, she thought. Something like this must be a daily occurrence, almost routine. "Not true?" Her voice wavered.

"I mean, you really haven't admired me from afar?"

Suddenly, a tiny prickle of anger goaded its presence beneath her scalp. She was tiring of all of this oral sparring. "Listen, if you're just going to stand there making fun of me . . ."

"No, no, really. I'm not." He chuckled lightly. "I am interested. I wouldn't have called if I weren't."

"What is it, just morbid curiosity?" Karen failed to understand why she was suddenly becoming so defensive. After all, she was the one who had initiated this whole thing. What had she expected?

"No, not at all. Besides, I like the sound of your voice."

Karen's knuckles grew pallid as she clutched the phone. "You do?" She said it in a weak, unusual voice.

"Yes, I do. And I'd like to meet you."

Karen mentally battled with herself. She wanted to tell him that she had met him today only hours ago. No, she decided. She couldn't let him know she was the nitwit who couldn't even give him the time.

"Could we meet sometime?" he asked.

"Yes, I think that can be arranged." She shuddered. Why, all of a sudden, she asked herself, did every word that came out of her mouth sound like a dialogue from a "B" movie?

"Do you ever go to the Pit on Willshire and Main?"

"Yes, I go there sometimes." Go there sometimes, she thought cynically. She had been there every day last week hoping she'd catch a glimpse of him.

"Could we meet there Monday after I get out of

track practice? Say about five-thirty?"

"Sounds great!" Mentally, she chastised herself for sounding so eager. "I mean . . . yes, I think I can make it."

"Good. I don't know who you are, so I suppose it's up to you to recognize me. Okay?"

"Okay."

"By the way, before I hang up, what's your name?"

"Karen," she replied, trying her best to sound casual.

"Mine's Marc . . . Marc Rodgers."

"Yes . . . yes, I know." How many times, over the last few weeks, had she said that name to herself?

"Okay, see you Monday then."

"Yes . . . Monday, five-thirty, at the Pit."

"Bye . . . Karen." A humming sounded as he hung up the phone.

Karen's wrist went limp as the weight of the receiver dropped it back onto the hook. Turning, she walked back into the living room as though she were in a hypnotic trance. A weak smile pulled at the corners of her lips.

Spike came bounding out of the kitchen a carrot poking from his mouth, his Government text tucked under his arm. "Ready to crack the books, Karen? We can get in about an hour. Your mom invited me for supper." He jostled her shoulder. She failed to react, staring vacantly across the room. "You know me when it comes to food. Besides, your mom is one of the best cooks west of the

Rockies." Pausing, his brows furrowed with concern as he peered closely into her face. "You all right? Your eyes look kind of glassy or something."

Karen, mechanically, sank down into the divan—a euphoric, yet placid expression coating her face. "Yes, Yes, I'm all right. Let's get started."

Spike dropped to the floor seating himself cross-legged in front of her still peering up into her face skeptically.

Chapter 3

Karen fidgeted nervously about on the smooth leather seat in the Pit. She had purposely chosen a back booth with the best vantage point of a view of the front entrance. The sights, sounds, and smells were the same as usual at the Pit. The greasy, tempting aroma of frying hamburgers and deep fat fried onion rings wafted through the air. The place teemed with high-school students milling about talking, laughing, and playing innocent tricks on one another. Karen watched them distractedly not really seeing any one particular face. A tinkling of silverware and a clatter of plates could be distinguished as the harried busboys cleaned vacant tables readying them for new occupants.

Out of the corner of her eye, Karen recognized many kids she knew and liked from school. Usually, she would have beckoned them to join her or would have been sought out to join them. Today, she looked away trying to remain anonymous. Today was a different day, a special day.

She looked about the walls populated with

posters of rock stars and teen idols. Raising up, she checked her hair in the flocked mirror above the fountain. She cringed. Her hair had never looked so bad in her entire life. Why had she set it last night? It looked tight, unnatural. Her blouse looked too new, too frilly, too pretentious, as though she wanted to make an impression. With splayed fingers she raked through her hair trying to loosen it. Another glance in the mirror failed to please her and she made a face at the reflection looking back at her.

A girl from across the room waved to her, smiling. Karen waved back feebly, without energy, not wanting to encourage her to come over. Out of the corner of her eye she saw the girl sober and toss her head haughtily. Karen couldn't blame her: it was a terrible way to act. She promised herself she would apologize tomorrow at school. She would tell her that she didn't feel well or something. She rationalized that it was true. She really didn't feel well at the moment.

Looking down at the soupy dish of ice cream, she moved her spoon through it vacantly. Her stomach swirled and for a moment she thought she was going to be sick. Bringing her glass of water to her lips, she sipped. It tasted flat and warm, the ice long since melted.

Glancing at her watch for the tenth time, she nervously tapped her fingers on the formica table top. Five-forty she reminded herself. He was already ten minutes late. Why had she ever put herself in such a position? A pang of fear charged through her as she looked up, examining the kids entering the front door. What if he didn't even show up? She could feel a self-debate emerging and felt that she didn't have the strength nor the patience for it. She tried to concentrate on filing a ragged edge of a fingernail. Why should he show up? No one liked girls who were that forward. And then again, he did take the time and bother to phone. That must prove something. He did sound as though he wanted to meet her. But, perhaps, it was a little game he played. Squealing, she sucked at the tip of her finger as the point of the file dug too deep beneath the nail. This was ridiculous. After all, he was just a boy. So what if he was the most handsome boy she had ever seen at Central High? So what if he had a voice that was as deep as a lion's roar? So what if he was a superb athlete?

At first, she had thought the weekend would never end. Her room was the cleanest it had been in years as she worked to keep her hands and mind occupied. Saturday night she had half-heartedly accepted a movie date with Eddie Graves and a coke afterward. She hadn't particularly cared about going out but she knew that if she stayed home she would just pace the floor and have a cardiac arrest every time the phone rang. Even throughout the movie her thoughts were on Marc Rodgers. When Eddie had slipped his arm around her shoulders, she was ashamed when she realized she was wondering what it would be like to have Marc do the same thing. And then on Sunday evening she had panicked when she realized that the weekend was practically over and she would have to finally face him. She had even thought of feigning that she was sick so she could stay home from school.

The Government exam had been a bear as Spike said it would and she knew she had gotten a terrible grade. Once, she had caught the stern, reproachful eyes of Mr. Price glaring at her as she gazed longingly out of the third-story window. The smells of spring invaded her nostrils and she had breathed deep, feeling anesthetized by them. An impatient clearing of the throat, by Mr. Price, had brought her back to reality and the impossible question about the Sixth Amendment to the Constitution.

Spike had hurried over to her after class with a worried look on his face. He had noticed that she was having difficulty concentrating. Innocently, she had passed it off as spring fever and asked him how he had done. Passing or failing the test didn't seem to matter to him; he was only concerned about her. Karen smiled to herself. Good, old, reliable Spike.

Karen lurched as a hand pressed into her shoulder. Swinging her head around, she looked up into Sandy's open, grinning face. At that moment she welcomed the friendly diversion and moved over to make room for her. Sandy was the only one she had told about this afternoon's rendezvous. Rendezvous, there goes that grade "B" dialogue again, she warned herself.

"Hasn't showed yet, huh?"

Karen shook her head trying to look unconcerned. "Probably stopped to buy me some candy or pick a bouquet of flowers."

"He'll be here. Don't worry." Sandy turned to her, pushing her glasses back up on her nose with a thumb, and smiled. "Who would pass up a date with the prettiest, most popular girl in school?"

"I'm not worried!" Karen snapped. She nipped the tip of her tongue realizing the words erupted too harshly, too explosively, too obviously. "It was a stupid thing to do anyway. A real kid's prank. It's like passing notes back and forth in grade school writing snotty little tidbits on them trying to shock each other." Karen jabbed a thumb in her chest. "I'm almost seventeen, for crying out loud! Isn't it time I grew up?" She extended her arms asking for an explanation to no one in particular. "Why, soon I'll be a senior and thinking about much more important, adult things like . . . what college I'm going to attend and what profession I'm going into. This is a kid's game." Shrugging her shoulders, she looked away.

"Well, just so you're not worried." Sandy peeked slyly out of the corner of her eye.

A snigger crept up Karen's throat as her cheeks puffed up, finally exploding. Both girls screamed with hilarity jabbing meekly at one another.

Just as she tried to sober, a side glance at Sandy sent her in hysterics once again. Finally, she dabbed at her cheeks with her handkerchief to remove the tears of mirth rolling down her face. Sighing, she leaned back against the cushioned seat. "I'm frantic! I've looked at my watch over a dozen times, sat here talking to myself, and about threw my purse into the mirror when I got a glance at my hair."

"Not to mention not eating your chocolate marshmallow ice cream. That, more than anything, describes how you feel." Sandy pointed at the pitiful-appearing dish.

Karen nodded and smiled. "I'm so thankful you showed up. I was about ready to go crazy sitting here imagining all sorts of things." With a fist, she tapped her friend on the shoulder.

"I was just going to come in and order me a peanut-butter parfait and drool over it and the handsome guy sitting with you," Sandy responded.

Karen looked at her skeptically. "I thought you were going on that diet starting today."

Sandy reared back her brows, arched in disbelief. "Did I say that? I must have been delirious. Besides, I still have a skirt and a pair of jeans that will still circumvent my waist," she said positioning her hands on her broad hips. Motioning to a waitress, Sandy ordered a parfait with extra nuts and whipped cream. "Mondays are always the best days to break diets. They're so depressing." During the first bite, Sandy's eyes bulged as she choked, hitting her spoon against the dish unable to speak.

Karen looked up with concern, raising her hand to dislodge the nut which had undoubtedly blocked her throat.

Mumbling unintelligibly, Sandy pointed her spoon toward the entrance.

Karen looked up to see Marc Rodgers hurriedly

entering, his eyes darting about searchingly. For a moment she had an uncontrollable urge to run, to escape. She didn't care how or where to; she just didn't want to meet him. Close up, he was even more handsome. Half-heartedly, she wished that it weren't so. Karen could see girls, throughout the Pit, stop abruptly in their conversations to turn and ogle him.

Sandy collected her wits and motioned toward the door. "Go on, do something before he gets away. I can tell by the way he's looking, he's trying to find you."

Sliding low in her seat, Karen suddenly felt pitifully drained. "I can't." Covering her eyes, she moved her head back and forth. "I can't explain it; I just can't. It's all I've thought about for weeks and now that I finally have a chance to meet him, I just can't."

"What do you mean, can't?" Sandy's voice sounded incredulous. "He's right here in the flesh!" She jumped to her feet and started pulling her from the booth.

Karen clutched a corner of the table refusing to move. In her mind, she could imagine how ridiculous and comical the two of them must appear.

Finally Sandy, totally exasperated, released her hand and made a beeline for the entrance. Karen gasped as she realized what she was planning on doing. Desperately, she groped toward her, flailing feebly at the air. Peeking between her fingers, she could see Sandy talking to Marc, gesticulating toward her emphatically. At that moment, she wanted to dissolve into oblivion.

Out of the corner of her eye she could see his face brighten and a shot of white, strong teeth. With long, confident strides, he advanced toward the booth.

Karen cringed, darting looks of revenge at Sandy who remained watching intently from the entrance.

Karen felt his presence before looking up at him.

"Miss 915-6773, I presume?"

The sound of his rich, full voice caused her pulse to quicken. She knew it must be visible to him. With a pitiful nod of her head she managed to look up into his blue eyes. "Yes," she tried to smile but the muscles in her face seemed frozen and it emerged more like an expression of pain.

"Marc Rodgers." He stuck out his hand.

Karen trembled as she felt her hand snuggle into his. "Hi," was all she managed to say.

"May I sit down, Karen?"

"Oh, sure." Never had she heard anyone pronounce her name so eloquently. She frowned as she noticed Sandy peering intently over her glasses trying to view every movement.

Marc slid into the cushioned seat opposite her. Karen could feel the heat of his eyes boring into her.

"Sorry I'm late. Track practice lasted longer tonight. We have a dual meet with Havenville Friday."

"That's okay." She winced, finding her voice thin and artificial.

"Would you like something? A coke or anything?"

"No. No, thank you." Furtively, she moved the dish of melted ice cream out of his line of vision. His eyes followed her hand across the table and behind the napkin dispenser.

"Not hungry?" He nodded slightly toward the soupy contents.

"No, not really." She shrugged shyly, placing her hands in her lap.

"I don't think you have anything to worry about as far as your weight. From what I can see from here, you're just right."

Karen could feel her face burning and knew her ears must be lit up to a point of illumination.

"Wait a minute!"

Karen looked up expectantly.

"Aren't you the girl who was out at the track Friday? The one I asked the time?"

Karen nodded feebly. "Yes, I'm afraid I must admit to that. You must've thought I was a complete idiot out there."

"Why?" he asked.

"Oh, no reason." Karen decided it would be best not to remind him of the fiasco with the wristwatch and her sudden transformation into a mute.

A long pause ensued as he sat across from her looking at her. Her heart raced and a flush coated her face as his eyes swept over her.

"Do you mind me telling you that you're a knock-out? I kind of figured you would be by the sound of your voice on the phone."

Karen licked her dry lips staring shyly down at the formica table top. "Thank you. That's really nice of you to say. I . . . I want you to know that I don't make a habit of leaving my telephone number in guys' cars. This is really the first time I've done a thing like that. I'm really very embarrassed about it."

Marc reached out laying his hand on her arm. "I know that. A good-looking girl like you wouldn't have to do that."

Her eyes looked down at his hand lightly grasping her arm and she suddenly felt much better. "Thank you again. Thank you for understanding."

He leaned forward and she could feel the warmth of his breath stroking her face. "I'm very glad you did what you did. Otherwise, we may never have had the chance to meet."

Karen smiled. He was just as nice as he was handsome, she thought to herself.

Sandy, a straw between her lips, craned her neck above the milling crowd to glimpse her friend. Karen was unaware of her stares this time as her eyes remained riveted to Marc's swarthy face. In her mind, she imagined him to have distant Greek or Mexican ancestry.

"Do you like it here? I mean, it must've been hard pulling up stakes during your senior year."

He nodded, a frown filtering across his handsome face as he stared down at the table. "My dad transferred and I had to go with my folks, that's all." He shrugged his broad shoulders, trying to make it sound trivial and unimportant. "It happens all of the time."

Karen caught a hint of subliminal regret as his voice assumed a tender sadness. "You must have left a lot of good friends behind." She winced. "Gee, I know it would be hard for me to leave Riverview. I've lived here all of my life." Mentally, she scolded herself, afraid he would now think she was common and homespun. She knew by his poise and maturity that he was urbane. "I . . . I suppose that sounds awfully dull to you."

He smiled, his eyes emitting a warm glow. "No, not at all. I think it's great to have roots. My family has lived all over the world. My dad, up until about a year ago when he retired, was an air force colonel. We've lived in parts of Asia and Europe." Hunching his shoulders, he suddenly seemed embarrassed. "I like good old U.S.A. best of course."

Karen sighed, looking dreamily toward the ceiling. "Oh, I think you are so lucky to be able to travel. I mean, to actually see all of the places that I've only read about in books would be terrific."

"It's pretty much the same the world over," he said matter-of-factly.

"Would you tell me some of the countries you've lived in?"

He thought for a moment. "Spain, Austria, France, in Europe, and Malaysia, and Indonesia, in Asia."

Increased wonder and admiration welled in Karen for this handsome, dark-haired boy. "I . . . I feel so . . . so insignificant," she finally managed to mutter.

Marc reached out and pressed her arm. "I don't see you that way, at all."

A deep, rosy hue crept up her throat and flooded into her face. For the moment she avoided his eyes, afraid she might display too much emotion knowing him such a short time.

"I did hate to leave California, though. It was great living there. I really dig surfing."

"Did you have to leave anyone special?" Instantly, she regretted the question. It seemed very forward as though she was pressing him too fast for answers. No annoyance was revealed in his eyes and she silently sighed with relief.

Lifting his hand from her arm, he dug self-consciously at a thumbnail. "I did leave someone I was very . . ." his composure seemed to become tenuous for a moment, ". . . very fond of, you might say."

"I'm sorry. If you don't want to talk about it, I'll understand."

"No, no," he said shaking his head. A thick shock of lustrous, black hair fell over his forehead making him look daring and a bit untamed. Karen felt herself being submerged in an unusual warmth. She shifted in her seat uncomfortably. She felt uneasy about the feelings she was experiencing due to the presence of this new boy in town.

"Lisa—."He looked up as though he needed to explain. "That was her name—and I were going steady. It tore us both up pretty badly when my dad's transfer came through."

"Do you still hear from her?" Karen was pulled from opposite poles hoping that he didn't yet feeling very selfish she felt this way.

"Yeah, but the letters are coming fewer and further between. I suppose pretty soon it'll be all over."

"I'm really sorry." She tried her best to appear sincere.

He shrugged, trying to look unconcerned. Karen was sure she could detect a distinct flicker of hurt in his deep blue eyes. "Oh, we're over two thousand miles apart so it's pretty hard to keep up a relationship." He cocked his head to one side and tried to smile. "That, and the fact that we're both still young and aren't really ready to commit ourselves yet."

"You haven't met anybody . . ." Karen hesitated trying to find the appropriate words without sounding totally brash, ". . . anybody here since you came."

He raised his eyes and looked at her. Her breath caught as her heart started to pound so wildly that she was afraid he would be able to hear it.

"Not until now."

Karen looked away afraid he would be able to distinguish the open exultation on her face. Her thoughts catapulted, colliding into one another as she tried to steady her voice to reply.

"I didn't leave my purse here, did I, Karen?"

Karen turned as Sandy looked down her nose inquisitively through her glasses. At that moment she was grateful her friend had intervened because things were happening too fast. She felt she needed time to think and collect her thoughts. She needed to go somewhere where it was quiet with no distractions. Some of her responses were foreign to her and frightened her.

"Isn't that a purse dangling from your arm, there?" Marc inquired.

Trying her best to look embarrassed, Sandy clamped a hand over her gaping mouth. "Oh, silly me. Sometimes, I am so empty-headed it's astounding." Her eyes caught Karen's revealing glance.

Karen nodded toward Sandy. "Marc, this is Sandy Benjamin, my best friend and composer of the note, I might add. Sandy, Marc Rodgers."

"Hi," he said. "We met briefly at the door a little while ago."

"Hi," Sandy responded. "I had to go over to you." She poked her hand forward in explanation. "We were afraid you'd get away." A pained expression contorted her smile as she looked toward Karen with apologetic eyes.

Karen shook her head and laughed. "It's okay, Sandy. We've already talked about it. Marc doesn't think I'm completely crazy."

"I don't think that at all." His eyes looked over to her, and Sandy immediately became aware that something had happened in the brief time that they had been together. Goose bumps popped out along her arms and she rubbed them abrasively, feeling suddenly chilled.

Turning his wrist, he glanced down at his watch and frowned. "Listen, I've got to go. My mom thinks the world will come to an end if we aren't sitting at the supper table promptly at six-thirty.

Could I drop you both off at home?" His question was directed to each of them but he looked at Karen only.

"I'd love to ride in that great car of yours, Marc, but I've got the Pumpkin."

"The what?" he asked, his full brows arched.

Sandy giggled. "That's what she calls her old, beat up VW. It resembles a discarded jack-o-lantern the day after Halloween."

Marc grinned and nodded. "That's too bad. I would've liked to run you both home. I've got a real mean machine out there."

"We know," Sandy said catching Karen's warning stare. "I mean, it would've been nice."

"Yeah, it's a great car," he said proudly. "It's got a 350 cubic inch V-8 Engine with J & E pistons, Crower valve gear and a 6-71 GMC roots-type super-charger topped off with dual carbs and mag wheels."

Karen and Sandy looked at each other quizzically as though he had suddenly lapsed into a foreign tongue. Karen swallowed, grasping for composure. "It sounds wonderful! I'd really like to ride in it sometime."

Marc extricated his large frame from the snug booth and grinned down at her. "You can bet on it. Okay if I call you tomorrow?"

"That . . . that would be great!" Karen had to force herself to control her elation.

At that moment she felt a hand reach from behind her to cover her eyes. She knew at once who it was. "Okay, Spike, cut the clowning."

He took his hand away and stuck it shyly into his back pocket. "How'd you know it was me?"

"How did I know?" Karen gasped disbelievingly. "You've pulled that stunt a thousand times on me in the last ten years."

Spike's face took on a flush and he shrugged. "Oh, yeah, I forgot." He looked around and winked. "How ya' doin', Sandy?"

"Real good, Spike," Sandy answered, looking up at him adoringly.

"Oh, I'm sorry," Karen said, looking toward Marc. "Spike, this is Marc Rodgers. Marc, this is Spike Marshall.

Spike assumed his charming boyish grin and reached for Marc's hand. Marc seemed to hesitate for a moment but finally took his hand, a slight tug at the corners of his mouth.

"Really great to meet you, Marc. I've been hearing exciting things all over school about the meet Friday. Everyone says it's going to be a toss-up between you and Riley from Havenville in the 1,500 meters."

Marc nodded. "Thanks, Spike. I've never seen Riley run, but I hear he's plenty good."

"From what I've heard you're no slouch either," Spike replied warmly.

"Well, I'll be out there doing my best."

"And we'll be out there watching you, Friday." He looked around to Karen and Sandy. "Right, you guys?"

They both nodded eagerly.

Marc checked his watch and grimaced. "Hey,

I've got to run; it's getting late. It's been really great meeting all of you." He smiled. "Until tomorrow then." He displayed his ivory-white teeth as he nodded to Sandy. His gaze lingered for several moments on Karen. Abruptly, as though he had to pull himself physically away, he turned and walked back through the crowd in the Pit and out the front entrance.

Sandy watched him leave and then crumpled into a seat opposite Karen emitting tiny, punctuated squeals of joy. "You did it! You really did it! He's everything you thought he was."

"And more . . . so much more," Karen added, still in a daze.

"Do you suppose he'll ask you out tomorrow? What do you think he'll say? Do you think you'll ride in his car? What?" Sandy's eyes rolled with excitement beneath her glasses.

Karen shrugged. "My answer is 'I don't know,' to all of the above four questions. All I know is, he's the greatest thing that's ever happened to me. He's everything I thought he'd be and more. He's . . . he's so mature. He's lived all over the world."

"This could be the big one, Karen. He could be Mr. 'It.' "

Karen looked over to her friend and grinned. "A girl could do worse, much worse."

"Hey, did you two forget about your old buddy, Spike, standing here totally in the dark?" He held his arms out in consternation.

Karen turned to him and pressed his arm. "Oh, I'm sorry, Spike. We didn't mean to neglect you."

"I guess my feelings will heal," he said purposely protruding a lower lip. "But, what I really want to know is, what's this Mr. 'It' business?"

"Oh, Spike," Sandy cried with excitement. "Karen's been trying to meet this guy for weeks. Finally, the other day we dropped a note into his parked car and he phoned her to meet him here today. Isn't that wild!"

A shocked expression came over Spike's face.

Karen looked down and studied the floor.

"You dropped a note into a guy's car! That's being pretty darned forward, isn't it, Karen?"

Karen's face flushed a bit, annoyed at Spike's rebuke. "Oh, for crying out loud, it was innocent enough. And look," she explained, "he turned out to be a really great guy."

Spike arched a speculative brow in thought.

"Come on, you guys," Karen said hurriedly before Spike could ask more questions, "let's go. I'll give you a ride home."

Together, they rose from the booth on their way out to the lot and to the Pumpkin.

Chapter 4

Karen struggled to concentrate on her studies the next day. During fourth period Spanish her mind wandered and she couldn't concentrate on the translations she was working on. Marc's image and voice continued to push its way into her thoughts. As Señor Gonzales continued to write and explain various Spanish phrases on the board, she wrote Marc's name in every describable way from fancy script to block print.

Glancing down at her watch, she sighed as she noted the time. There were still two more hours before the dismissal bell. How would she survive? How could she possibly tolerate two more hours of class? Already, she had decided to skip cheerleading practice after school in case Marc decided to call. She knew Miss Lathrop would be unhappy about it but she wanted to be home near the phone.

Karen realized that she was being ridiculously obvious but also realized that she couldn't help it. It was as though a huge tidal wave was sweeping her along no matter how she struggled against it.

She was taking no chances of losing him now that they had finally met. Marc was in her thoughts night and day. He was her last thought before she fell asleep and the first when she awoke. She could feel her entire existence being consumed by this handsome, magnetic new boy in town. At times, it was an uncomfortable, helpless feeling, as though she had no control over her own will or destiny. This was a new experience for her. Up until this point she had always been in control. This was one thing she was always proud of.

An unrecognizable gibberish of Spanish words mingled in the background of her thoughts. Once, she glanced up and noticed a smattering of hands held high to answer a question. She smiled uncomfortably to herself realizing that she didn't know the question, much less the answer. At that moment, Spanish seemed unimportant, almost trivial, compared to everything else. Right now, Marc's call was the only important thing, the only thing that really mattered.

"Señorita Cooper, Yo hablo Español?"

Karen lurched as the sound of her name punctured the translucent shield of her mind. Looking up, she noticed the many suspicious smiles on the faces of her classmates.

"Let me repeat myself, Señorita Cooper," Señor Gonzales reiterated, his smooth black brows arching, skeptically. "Yo hablo, Español?"

"Si," Karen replied weakly.

"Would you care to expand on that, Señorita Cooper?" Señor Gonzales asked.

Karen cleared her throat feeling the hot, sticky flames of embarrassment lick at her ears beneath her hair. "No . . . no, sir."

"I see. It would appear, Señorita Cooper, that you feel no need to learn the phrases on the board." He tapped the chalkboard with the end of a yardstick. "This is Spanish II fourth hour, not doodling II fourth hour, I believe. I would appreciate your attention the remainder of the period."

Karen nodded. "I'm sorry, Mr. Gonzales."

"Señor Gonzales," he reminded her.

"Señor Gonzales," she corrected herself. "I'll pay more attention."

Señor Gonzales executed a slight bow of acknowledgement in her direction. "Thank you, Señorita Cooper." Turning to the board, he hit at the next phrase. "All right, altogether . . ."

Much to her relief, everyone's attention turned from her back to the board as she focused her's there as well. Sandy looked back from her seat near the front of the room and shrugged quizzically. Karen returned the shrug and perfunctorily repeated the phrases as Señor Gonzales pointed to them.

At last, the sound of the bell sliced through the last oral phrase and everyone bolted toward the exit. Karen hurriedly worked her way into the middle of the throng willing to get bumped and buffeted about to escape Señor Gonzales' almost certain interrogation.

Sandy caught up with her halfway down the hall

on the way to English Literature III. "Hey, hold up. I never saw you in that much hurry to get to old Pinky's class before. You finding the 'to be's' or 'not to be's' are starting to turn you on?"

Karen turned, smiling at the familiar voice. "No it's still a drag. We're reading *Antony and Cleopatra.*"

Sandy wrinkled her nose in distaste.

"Old Cleo was quite a gal, Sandy. She had Antony wrapped around her little finger." She rolled her eyes. "Not similar to my situation with my Marc, I can assure you."

Sandy swiped her shaggy bangs out of her eyes and placed a hand on her friend's shoulder. "He'll call. Good grief, school's not even out yet. Give the guy a chance."

Karen nodded her submission. "I know I'm acting like a royal idiot, but I just can't think of anything else."

Sandy shook her head, her mouth set taut. "You've got it hard, kid. Even worse than Mr. Briar back in junior high. I've never seen you quite this way before."

"I know," Karen said dejectedly. "If it wasn't so wonderful it would be terrible." She hit her forehead with the palm of her hand. "Will you listen to me? I'm now talking in riddles. Next thing you know, I'll be hallucinating."

"He'll call! He'll call! He said he would and he will. Have a little faith, Karen."

"I've never wanted anything more in my life than this, Sandy. He's just got to call."

"He said he would, didn't he?"

Karen nodded.

"Okay, he will," Sandy said with a punctuated movement of her head as though the explanation was final. "Now, just relax and get back to the land of the living."

Karen smiled weakly. "You're right. If I don't have that much faith and trust in him, what kind of relationship would it be anyway?"

"Right! By George, I think you've got it," Sandy replied in a thick Cockney accent.

A sea of students jammed the halls talking, laughing, and maneuvering their way to their fifth hour classes. Karen and Sandy crowded themselves flush to a row of gray, metallic lockers to prevent being trampled upon. Suddenly, Karen's eyes enlarged and she bobbed her head from side to side trying to peer through the myriad of faces and bodies herding down the hall. She waved wildly, her face alight.

Sandy looked at her with a doubtful expression on her face as she nudged her glasses back up on her nose. "What? What's the matter with you?"

"I saw him!"

"Who? Marc? You saw Marc?"

Karen nodded her head still trying to look through the jostling bodies. She pointed up the hall. "Isn't that the back of his head going on down the west wing? He's tall like Marc and his hair is just as black."

"I really don't know," Sandy replied apathetically. "I've really never studied the back of his head."

Karen's shoulders slumped and she sighed as the boy turned the corner disappearing from view. "I know that was him. He looked right at me when he got to the top of the stairs. I know he saw me waving at him. He just ignored me." She shrugged and kicked at the polished corridor floor. "He didn't wave or even smile."

"You're right, kid. I think you are starting to hallucinate. Every guy you see from now on over six feet tall with black hair is going to cause you to break out in a cold sweat." Sandy peered intently down the hall. "I didn't see him. But, of course, I'm not looking for him as hard as you are."

Karen shook her head. "I know it was him. He didn't even wave or smile."

Sandy brought her hands up to her full hips and frowned. "Listen, you've got to get hold of yourself. You look like you're about to crumble."

Students seemed to evaporate down long corridors, hurrying down stairs, and disappearing into doorways. The loud tumult lowered to a mumble and then, in sequence, into abrupt silence as the tardy bell clanged its warning. The two girls stood alone, still backed against the lockers, checking their watches with dread.

"I've got to get to Home Ec. Lacey has a fit if we're a split-second late. Listen, I'll call you after school." Sandy turned and darted down the hall.

"No! Don't call me!" Karen shouted as they scurried in opposite directions.

"Okay. But why?"

"Marc might try to get me. I don't want the phone tied up."

"Gotcha," Sandy yelled back, just a wave of her hand visible as she disappeared around a corner.

Karen darted breathlessly through the doorway and rushed to her seat. Her thoughts were preoccupied as she failed to take note of Mr. Pinkerton's disgruntled squint as she flung herself into her seat.

Karen's eyes remained transfixed with manic intensity on the phone sitting before her on the coffee table. Immediately, upon arriving home, she rushed into the hall and seated herself next to it. After staring an hour at the plastic, inanimate object, she returned to her room to change her clothes, her ears attuned to the slightest jingle.

Once, it rang and she surged forward to answer it. Abruptly, she warned herself to wait at least until it had rung three times. After all, she didn't want him to know she was practically perched on top of it. The moment of propriety had mattered little for it had been Mrs. Percell who wanted to talk to her mother about the upcoming church bazaar. Karen knew of the lady's verbosity and was thankful that her mother had not been home yet.

Finally, Karen took the phone into the living room and plugged it into an extension outlet. At least, she assured herself, she could do some homework while she waited. Concentration on geometry was futile. She struggled with the words of Shakespeare in English Literature. The words were empty as she read and reread each line trying to extract the meaning. With a groan, she slammed her books closed, tucked her stocking feet beneath her, and stared down at the phone.

At one point, she tried to influence it to ring by will alone, mind over matter. She had seen it done by a psychic on TV. She never really believed in such phenomenon and felt ridiculous but, at this point, was willing to try anything.

When that failed, she decided to get some appointed chores accomplished and found herself glancing over her shoulder at the phone as she dusted the furniture. Once, she checked with the operator to be sure that it was in working order; she was assured that it was. After she hung up, she hit herself on the side of the head with frustration realizing Mrs. Percell had called not an hour ago.

Karen winced biting into her lip as she checked the time—6:15. Why hadn't he phoned? Why was he torturing her this way? From the kitchen she could hear the busy bustling of her mother preparing dinner. The clatter of plates and the metallic banging of pans raked at her already raw nerves. With a deep sigh, she ambled sullenly toward the kitchen.

Mrs. Cooper turned, smiling, wiping her damp hands on her apron. "Dear, would you make a salad for dinner? Your father should be driving in in about fifteen minutes."

Karen nodded without replying and walked with little enthusiasm to the refrigerator.

"How was your day? I noticed you got right to your homework after school." She nodded to herself. "I think that's a good policy, Karen."

Karen pulled open the vegetable bin and brought out a solid, green head of lettuce. With overly emphatic movements, she tore the cellophane wrap from it and broke it in half. She was unaware of the obvious anger her actions displayed.

Mrs. Cooper laid a paring knife aside and looked at her daughter, a frown settling over her face. Her "ESP and x-ray eyes" were at work again.

"Anything wrong, Karen?"

"No, nothing," Karen replied without turning around.

A motherly, understanding expression came to Mrs. Cooper's face as she walked over to her daughter and placed an arm around her shoulders. "Dear, sit down and tell me about it. It's written all over your face that there is definitely something wrong."

Karen shrugged her mother's arm away. "Really, mom, everything's fine."

Mrs. Cooper cupped Karen's chin and looked into the eyes starting to glaze with tears. "Is there anything I can do to help? I know something's wrong."

In that instant the flood of emotion which Karen had struggled to contain all day rushed forward from its constraints and peaked. "Oh, mom, do you always have to be so right! Can't you just be wrong once in your life?" Karen's voice, which had started off soft and uncertain, ended in a brittle wail, surprising her. Mentally, she kicked herself as she looked at the hurt flooding over her mother's face.

"I . . . I didn't mean to pry, Karen. I just thought

perhaps it might do you some good to talk about it. Sometimes, it helps to share your burdens with others. It makes the load easier." Her voice remained bland and placid, almost beseeching. "If you'd rather not talk about it that's all right, too. Just remember, I'm here if you want to." With a reassuring smile, she turned back to her chores at the kitchen counter.

Karen looked down at the blurred image of the lettuce as tears seeped from the corners of her eyes and rolled down her flushed cheeks. Over and over she repeated to herself to get control. It didn't seem to matter. She couldn't remember when she had felt so empty, so futile.

Karen looked down as she felt a tug on her hand. Dody was bent forward in an effort to pull her toward the living room. She giggled, thinking Karen's resistence was part of the game she was playing.

"Come see the funny clown on TV, Karen." She grimaced as she looked around pointing at her nose. "He's got a big red nose that looks like a Christmas light and long, floppy feet." A giggle vibrated in her throat. She tugged at Karen's hand once again. "Come see, before he's gone."

Karen snatched her hand from Dody's grasp. "I don't want to see it! You go ahead and watch it. I've got to help mom with dinner." She turned her back and walked to the table.

Not to be denied, Dody rushed to her pulling at her skirt. "No! No! Hurry, Karen! He's real funny. He falls down all the time. Hurry, or he will be gone."

Karen shook her head, continuing to shred the lettuce.

"Please, Karen. Hurry before he goes away. Please! Please!"

With a warning scowl on her face, Karen swung around grabbing Dody by the shoulders. Dody's head bandied about as Karen shook her. "I said I didn't want to see it! Now, you get in there and leave me alone!"

Dody's smile disappeared from her face. She turned and walked slowly back to the living room with her head bowed and her hands stuck deeply into her jeans' pockets. Now and then she glanced warily over her shoulder.

Karen stood there feeling the shame mount within her. Abruptly, she turned back to the salad. Once, she caught the hurt, worried eyes of her mother watching her.

Karen lay on her bed in the darkened room staring blankly at the ceiling. She knew that all tears had been spent. A nauseous, empty feeling pervaded throughout her being. The tick of the alarm clock on her nightstand throbbed in her brain. With a sick groan, she rolled to her side to gaze at the luminous numerals—12:45 A.M.

Marc hadn't called. What a fool she was lashing out at her mother and Dody, sitting mute and motionless during dinner, shifting her salad about on her plate. No boy was worth this. Why had he ever moved to Riverview? she asked herself. Confusion swirled in her brain. Perhaps, something came up preventing him from phoning. Sitting up, she hit at her pillow with her fist as though it suddenly had become her enemy. Who was she kidding? This wasn't Outer Mongolia. A person could always get to a phone if he really wanted to. Marc Rodgers just didn't want to, that's all.

Chapter 5

During the remainder of the week Karen floated through the days not totally aware of her existence. She had seen Marc between classes but he didn't speak to her or even mention not calling. She went to class and stared blankly at the instructors, hearing their words but not absorbing the lessons they tried to teach. Pop quizzes were handed in without an attempt at the answers. Her usual buoyancy faded into lassitude and indifference. Karen's parents, friends, and teachers could recognize the change in her but thought it was temporary and the "old Karen" would soon return. After all, they rationalized, spring fever affects everybody once in a while.

Sandy's support and light banter tried but failed to pull her from her gloom. Up until now, she had always been successful with funny faces, or jokes to prod her friend into hilarity even at her worst depths of depression. But now, Karen would politely smile, still aware of their friendship, and then return to her despair. Sandy openly admitted that she was worried; this was worse. This was different from her other "infatuations." She missed Karen and the fun and comradery that they shared.

Only Dody managed to get a genuine smile from Karen. When she snuggled close to her on the divan in the evening, Karen felt better. She knew that Dody wouldn't demand an explanation or query her on what was the matter. Dody never made any demands on anyone.

The birds chirped their spring song. Sweet smells of lilacs and honeysuckle filled the air. Gentle, warm breezes moved the lush-leaved branches of the trees. Karen walked in a slow, shuffling gait toward home, her head bowed, staring vacantly at the sidewalk. Each step seemed a supreme effort. Today, she had decided to neither drive the Pumpkin nor take the bus; she was looking forward to the solitude of the long walk.

A hard ball obstructed her throat as she swallowed. She thought back to the two times she had seen Marc Rodgers at school. Once, he had turned a corner in the hall and practically run into her between classes. He had apologized for his clumsiness as though she were a complete stranger. Karen had stood there anticipating a word, a smile, but he had merely shrugged and hurried off to his class. The other incident had occurred yesterday, in the school cafeteria. Marc had been sitting at a corner table with Lori Mobley. The two of them were laughing and talking animately, obviously enjoying each other's company. Karen felt the pangs of jealousy wrench within her as she stared in their direction. Lori had a "reputation" with the boys at Central High. What was he doing with her? Of course Lori was pretty, full-figured, and spirited. Her parents were overly liberal believing that she was now old enough to take charge of her own life. From what Karen had observed and heard, Lori was anything but in control. Before now, Karen had always felt a little sorry for her knowing that if parents really care they do place restrictions on their children. It was a "cop out" to be too lenient. As Karen watched the two of them together, she was ashamed of the bitter, almost acrid feeling toward Lori. At that very moment, she wanted to hurry over there and tell Marc what kind of girl she was; she wanted to warn him of her reputation. Suddenly, she had looked away feeling more than foolish. Marc obviously knew about Lori. He was a big boy and he certainly didn't need her to counsel his life. Anyway, she knew that her motives were selfish. She would not be doing it for his good, but for her own.

A sudden, deafening roar nudged at her heels and she looked up to see the dust ballooning skyward and then settling back to the pavement. Turning, Karen looked up into the smiling, mottled face of Spike Marshall. His pale blue eyes looked out from beneath the motorcycle helmet he wore low over his brow. His warm, infectious smile comforted her for the moment and she strangely welcomed his presence.

"The Pumpkin on the blink?" he yelled over the deep, punctuated rumble of his cycle.

Karen shook her head walking to the curb. "No, I just felt like walking today."

The machine purred as it idled with a subtle vibration beneath the red-haired boy.

Spike pulled the gold-flecked, fiberglass helmet from his head and mopped an arm over his sweaty brow. He grinned, exhibiting a perfect set of white teeth. "Want a lift? I'm on my way to watch the track meet between Central and Havenville High. Got to support the jocks, you know." He chuckled.

Karen hesitated a moment fully aware that Marc would be participating in the meet. She debated whether she wanted to punish herself further, sitting on the sidelines yearning for his attention but receiving only his indifference. Glancing up, she looked into Spike's eyes as he patiently waited for her decision. There would be no benefit in shutting herself off from life by going home and secluding herself behind four walls like a recluse. Even if Marc Rodgers had decided to ignore her she had to go on living. Finally, Karen smiled and nodded. "Sure, let's go. Just like you said, we should give the jocks our support." She hopped on the cycle, straddling it, and without a thought encircled Spike's waist. For an instant, just before he jammed the bike into gear, she felt a subtle tingle charge through her as she felt the solid muscle and sinew of her old friend through his T-shirt. Involuntarily, she loosened her grasp not understanding this unusual reaction.

"Hold on!" Spike yelled to her over his shoulder.

Instantly, a pall lifted from Karen and she felt strangely excited. She couldn't count the many times she had ridden on Spike's Honda "250" but today, for some reason, it was different. It felt comfortable and she could detect the dark cloud, which had hovered over her all week, start to fade. This old friend had known that she was unhappy and he was there. He was there not with long harangues or sage advice but just there with his presence assuring her that he would help if he possibly could. Spike had always been there when she needed him, as was Sandy. Karen suddenly felt ashamed as she thought how she always took both of them for granted.

For the first time in weeks she started noticing the world around her again. As they sped along saying nothing to each other, she smiled watching kids playing ball in the park, a lady bent over pulling weeds from her flower bed, two women pushing carriages exchanging talk about motherhood. It was there, all there. There was so much more to life than pining away for a person who didn't even know you existed.

Her hair blew back in an auburn stream. She didn't worry that it would be in a mess when they stopped; Spike didn't seem to care. He seemed to be just as attracted to her in a sweatshirt and jeans as in a chiffon evening gown. It was the person he liked, not the wrapping. Karen breathed in the pungent, fresh smells of spring grateful to be young and alive.

Spike wrenched the handlebars in a sharp arc

and bolted down the shady, tree-lined avenue leading to the stadium. Havenville's red and white banners and Central's Blue and Gold had been hoisted atop metal poles declaring the event. They could be heard as they flapped and snapped in the breeze. Two yellow school buses, boldly stenciled with the rival school's district number, were parked in the lot.

Inside the stadium, the discus, javelin, and shot put events were under way and clusters of supporters from each school were congregated at each place.

Karen's pulse quickened as she heard the distant, spontaneous cheers of excitement as well as moans of despair as athletes achieved or failed on their attempts. She cheered loudly for many of Central High's athletes. The spirit and thrill of competition had always been in her blood and she felt suddenly charged with excitement. For the moment, all thoughts of Marc Rodgers were gone.

Karen watched, fists clenched her muscles rigid, mentally pushing the high-jumpers over the bar. When a Central High athlete cleared seventeen feet eight inches in the pole vault on his third attempt, she catapulted into the air her arms stretched skyward. She celebrated by embracing Spike in a strong, excited hug.

From the press box a hollow voice announced over the loudspeaker that the field events were now culminating and the running events would start. Looking over Spike's shoulder she could see the many male athletes pull off warm-ups going immediately into various muscle-limbering exercises. Her eyes searched the blue and gold colors. Her heart leaped for a moment as she recognized the tall, straight stature of Marc Rodgers, stripping out of his "sweats," rapidly touching his toes. She watched, mesmerized, as his sleek, perfectly honed body went through its limbering routine. Once, Karen was sure, he had seen her as he looked up from his sit-ups. The black shock of hair hung impishly over his forehead making him appear even more charming. Karen looked away embarrassed and cringed as she suddenly realized that she was still clinging to Spike. Quickly, she released her grasp and stepped back her face glowing.

"I'm . . . I'm really sorry, Spike."

"About what?"

"For nearly choking you to death. I get too excited sometimes."

Spike grinned and shrugged. "You don't see me complaining, do you?"

Karen looked up at the freckled, red-haired boy and smiled. "You never complain, Spike. I wish I could always be on top of the world like you. You never get depressed or seem to have a worry or care."

"Have you really taken time to notice, Karen?" A strange, crooked smile came to his lips.

"I don't know what you mean."

Spike waved his hand as though he were trying to erase his last statement. "Ah, forget it. The main thing is that you're happy again. What say you let me buy you a Coke and we'll get a good seat for the running events. I hear this new guy is dynamite in the 1,500 meters."

Karen looked up at him quizzically. Had he said that intentionally to test her reaction? Looking into his open, smiling face she quickly dismissed her suspicions. "Sounds like a good idea. Tell you what, I'll race you over to the concession stand. By the time you get those big clodhoppers off of the ground I'll be sipping a Coke and have half a hot dog eaten."

"Oh, yeah?" Spike called back. "Listen, I may not be poetry in motion but I can still beat those short, stubby legs of yours."

Karen pummeled him on the arm, playfully. "Short and stubby, is it? This race is going to be like the tortoise and the hare and guess who you are?"

"I hope the tortoise." He grinned. "Because he's the smart one."

With an exasperating push to his chest, Karen bolted forward with a shriek. Plunging toward the concession stand she was weak with laughter hearing his anguished breathing and heavy feet drumming closely behind her. Finishing just yards ahead of him, she quickly assumed a relaxed stance, propping her chin up with a fist on the corner of the concession stand. As he puffed breathlessly up beside her she feigned a yawn as though she were bored waiting for him.

"You had a head start," he stammered trying to catch his breath. "That's unfair!"

"But remember, Superstar, I've got those short,

stubby legs. I am at a distinct disadvantage."

His freckled face wrinkled and he burst into laughter, jostling her shoulder.

Together they stood in the canopied shade nibbling on hot dogs and swigging thirstily on cold drinks. Just as Spike popped the last bite of bun into his mouth, he slyly dumped the remainder of the ice down her neck. Karen's eyes bulged and her breath caught as she shrieked in shocked discomfort. A mischievous glint came to her eyes and the look signaled for him to make a hurried exit. Again, he ran from pillar to pillar beneath the stadium trying to avoid the threat of receiving ice down his neck.

They were, once again, like two special friends. Karen's spirits soared as she teetered back and forth trying to grab him peeking out on the other side of the concrete post.

Spike moaned as he felt the ice slither down his neck and over his chest. An involuntary quake wracked through him as the ice left its frigid trail.

At last, they both leaned against the pillars exhausted, choking back the tears of mirth.

A brassy voice boomed from the speaker above their heads. It announced the last call for the fifteen-hundred meter participants. Spike stared up at the metal box and waved feebly toward it. "Suppose we'd better get out there and find a seat. This is supposed to be the best contest of the day. The new guy is supposed to be an even match for Riley of Havenville. Everyone says they'll probably compete neck and neck."

Karen looked abruptly away afraid that he would read the anxious expression on her face. For an instant she had an urge to take Spike's hand and pull him toward his cycle. She didn't want to see Marc Rodgers any more today. She decided, perhaps, it would be best if she never saw him again. For the first time in days, she felt good. Karen wanted to carry on her life with her family and friends minus any intervention from the new boy in town.

Spike stared at her quizzically. "You still here, Karen? You look like you've been a million miles away."

Karen looked up and smiled warmly. "Maybe I have. Maybe it's time I came home for good."

Spike shrugged and grinned. "That's too heavy for me." His light brows arched in bewilderment. "Way too heavy for me."

Karen shook her head. "Never mind, Spike. It doesn't matter any more. You're right." She nodded toward the track entrance. "Maybe we should get going so we get a good seat."

Spike encircled her shoulders and they walked toward the track; he had accepted the vague, unintelligible explanation at face value. Karen was so grateful that he had asked no questions.

The thin-clad athletes were lined in staggered lanes. Some were still doing limbering exercises. Others were running in place shaking their arms nervously. Karen avoided looking at the tall, dark boy in the outside lane. Even without realizing it, her palms were moist as she gripped the railing.

A dull, punctuated blast of the pistol acknowledged the start of the race and the crowd, spontaneously, rose to its feet cheering, anticipating a duel between the superb athlete from Havenville and the new boy, Marc Rodgers.

Karen's attention was drawn to him even though she mentally fought against it. She begrudgingly felt a shiver reverberate through her. Even from a distance, she could tell that he was someone special. His gait was smooth and effortless the first 440 staying a few carefully measured strides behind his rival. Soon, the other four sprinters expended themselves after two laps and quickly lagged far behind. It was obvious that the race would have only two main participants.

Karen visored her eyes staring directly into the sun at the tall, lean, swarthy figure running like a well-precisioned machine on the opposite side of the track. Even from where she sat she could see the solid knots of muscle bulging from his calves as he stretched his legs to take advantage of every inch in each stride.

The Havenville boy was ahead as they came into the far turn of the third lap. His body was flushed and dripping with sweat; a grimace of pain coated his face. Each stride now seemed difficult, belabored. In radical contrast, Marc Rodgers glided along with a relaxed, placid expression, seeming to enjoy the contest. There was not a trace of discomfort on his handsome face. It appeared to the spectators that he was out for an evening jaunt and, just by accident, it had turned into competition. The muscles lining his shoulders glistened with moisture emphasizing their deliniation. Karen looked away as he passed closely by the bleachers where she was sitting.

As the two athletes neared the last turn the pace quickened. The agonizing strain was etched on the Havenville boy's flushed face. Marc Rodgers, with precise syncronization, slid into an accelerated gear and gained dangerously on his faltering opponent. Karen clutched the railing until her knuckles were pallid as the new boy drew up even with his rival. Only ten yards from the finish line Marc moved easily past him breaking the tape. It was all Karen could do to keep from shouting with joy as the crowd roared to its feet with appreciation. The Havenville athlete stumbled across the finish line his chest heaving torturously. The crowd gasped in unison as he fell forward and collapsed to the ground.

Marc Rodgers positioned his hands on his lean hips and walked around the track to the cadence of the crowd's cheers and adulation. Karen couldn't help the goose bumps that popped out all over her bare arms. It was announced, excitedly, that a new league record had just been set!

"That was quite a race, huh, Karen?" Spike turned his head toward her noticing at once the dazed expression on her face. He might as well not even have been there. At that moment, her attention was entirely with the tall, dark lad receiving plaudits across the track. Inwardly, Spike recoiled as he could see the magnetic attraction in her eyes the new boy had for her.

"Did you say something, Spike?" Her eyes on Marc.

The cheers increased as he jogged around to the forefront of the track his arms thrust skyward in a gesture of victory. The Havenville athlete, still lying on the ground, was almost ignored with the exception of his coach and trainer bent over his heaving, writhing body.

Karen watched as he received congratulations and pats on the back from coaches and teammates and then easily pulled his sweat pants over his lean, muscular legs. A lump churned in the depth of her stomach and then found an unfamiliar route to her throat. Tears of longing welled in her eyes and then coated them completely and she saw him through a watery blur. Furtively, she muffed at her nose with an upturned palm afraid Spike would see the emotional strain she was going through. Looking bashfully away from him, she struggled to speak. "Could . . . could we go now, Spike? I really should get home."

Spike turned to her at once noticing the unusual blush of her cheeks as well as a lone, unleashed tear racing from the corner of an eye. "Sure. Sure, we can go right now." Realizing that she needed comforting, he awkwardly placed his arm around her shoulder and easily directed her up the steps to the exit.

"Karen! Karen . . . wait!"

Spike felt the girl wrench around at the sound of the call.

Karen bit into her lip with ecstasy and disbelief as she saw Marc raise his hand and beckon to her. She stopped and stared, scarcely breathing, as he ran toward her hurdling the iron railing with ease and then running up the steps to her. Spike dropped his arm and positioned it behind his back as though, suddenly, his rights had been withdrawn.

Swiping at her tears, Karen managed a smile at the handsome, dark youth staring up at her from three steps below with his entrancing blue eyes shrouded with the black swooping lashes.

"I . . . I thought it was you," he gasped trying to catch his breath. "I really . . . want to talk to you."

A thousand doubts, a thousand questions hurled themselves at her all at one time. But, for the moment, he was here right next to her and that was all that mattered. "That was a wonderful race, Marc. The crowd just went wild. That guy from Havenville has never been beaten up until now."

"Yeah, that was a thriller right down to the wire," Spike interjected. "Congratulations!"

Marc looked coldly at the mottled-faced boy without saying a word.

Spike enthusiastically offered his hand to the athlete. At that same moment Marc twisted his head around his attention drawn away abruptly. He craned his neck over the crowd to watch a group of athletes line up for the 880 relay. Spike, feeling a bit foolish, finally withdrew his hand and wiped it self-consciously alongside his jeans, finally depositing it in his jacket pocket.

Marc returned his attention and gaze to Karen. "Listen, Karen, I can get away from here in about five minutes. Like I said, I really need to talk to you. Could I give you a lift home or something?" His eyes looked up at her imploringly.

Karen realized that there would be no way she would be able to resist a request made by this handsome new boy. But, in this instance, she didn't want to seem overly obvious, overly eager. "I . . . I don't know, Marc. I think things have changed in the past week. We . . . we can't just start over as though nothing has happened."

He looked up at her with a flash of flawless, white teeth. "Let's go somewhere to talk."

Karen could feel the hot rush of embarrassment flood her face. She could also feel her spirits lift and soar as the reality came plummeting through her that their relationship was still alive. Suddenly, she turned to Spike who feigned interest in the race proceeding down on the track. He was standing with his hands jammed into his jacket pockets. Little did she realize that they were balled into fists. "I . . . I came with Spike on his cycle. I really should . . ." She looked up at her old friend and winced. "Would you mind if Marc took me home? I think there's a couple of things that both of us need to get settled.

A deep, reddish hue emerged over Spike's freckled face as he bit into his lower lip battling to contain his rage. "No, no go ahead." He tried to shrug carelessly.

Karen swung her head toward Marc. A moment

of perplexity goaded at her. Reaching toward Spike, she pressed his shoulder warmly. "Thanks, Spike. I really appreciate your understanding."

Spike's pale, bluish-green eyes looked down at her and she cringed for a moment as they seemed piercing. "That's me, good old understanding, Spike." Hunching his shoulders, he pulled on his fiberglass cycle helmet and turned continuing to walk toward the exit.

"I'll see you later, Spike," Karen yelled after him. She noticed his hand being raised feebly in acknowledgment as he disappeared through the wide, cavernous exit.

Karen's heart pounded in her ears and a wave of vertigo swept through her brain at the quick turn of events. She looked down at Marc's dark hand wrapped tightly around hers and smiled. She didn't want to think of anything right now, but the moment, this moment when Marc and she were together again.

Chapter 6

Marc sat across the table his hand touching Karen's. Every time they started to talk an admirer would interrupt to congratulate him on his fantastic feat this afternoon. His eyes seemed to scintillate with excitement, Karen thought. At times, she thought, she would inflate with pride at being seated opposite this handsome, charismatic boy.

The atmosphere, in the Pit, was even more chaotic than usual with everyone celebrating the resounding victory over Havenville High and over Riley in particular. It was a day to rejoice and everyone was taking advantage of it. The noise and pandemonium beat at her brain. Karen heard it and was physically present in the midst of it, but yet was only conscious of Marc's hand warmly clasping hers. At one moment, he stood up on the bench raising his hands to the ceiling and received applause and accolades from the teeming throng of high schoolers. A subtle flush coated his face as he was obviously enjoying his moment of triumph.

Sounds of laughter, shouting, cheers, and a busy

background of continuing business assaulted Karen's ears but she enjoyed each second of it.

Marc looked around, waving enthusiastically to a group of students in a far corner. "My grateful public, you know. A celebrity never has any peace."

Karen nodded with a smile but cocked a brow not quite certain just how much was in jest. She sipped at her Coke watching him go from table to table to quip with friends and to continue to receive plaudits. Finally, she sank back against the padded leather seat, folded her arms, and waited for him to return to the booth.

"Sorry, Karen," he said breathlessly, "they just won't leave a guy alone. I guess I gave all of them quite a thrill today."

Looking up, Karen smiled warmly. "Yes, you really did. It's a great day for Riverview."

Clenching his fist, he thrust it forward as a group of students passed the booth. Karen noticed a few frowns of consternation on some of the faces who obviously didn't share the thrill of victory as did the others.

"Marc," she said trying to coax him back to her, "could we maybe talk a little bit about last week?"

Suddenly, a frown of seriousness shaded his face. His dark-blue eyes turned to her giving her complete attention. Reaching across the table, he clasped her hand warmly. "I'm sorry. I guess I've been kind of neglecting you, haven't I?"

"Oh, no! I understand how you feel. This is a real special day for you. You don't beat a league record every day, you know." She tried to smile but found that her facial muscles felt taut, unyielding.

Marc shook his head vehemently. "No! Listen, I've been thinking about you all week and now that you're here, I'm neglecting you." He hit his palm against his forehead. "I'm a real dope sometimes."

Karen pressed his hand. "No, you're not! You have just been preoccupied, that's all." Her arms made a wide arc. "Gee, how could anyone blame you with everyone singing your praises about your win and every girl in the Pit ready to lie down at your feet."

A lip curled under slightly in a subtle pout. His eyes lowered and the long lashes provided a canopy over them. "You make me sound as if my head is getting so big that I'd never be able to find a hat big enough to fit it."

. Karen's voice broke in her urgency to make an appeasement. "Oh, no! Marc, I didn't mean that at all. I understand how it must be for you." She displayed a palm in explanation. "A new guy comes to town. He is handsome, nice, and a great athlete. Naturally, he is going to be a big hit with everyone, especially with the girls."

Slowly, he raised his eyes, a smile lighting his face, a hint of smugness pulling at the corners of his mouth. "I don't think I affect the girls that way, Karen. I just try to be myself, that's all."

"And that's what does it." She shrugged, looking shyly down at the table absentmindedly tracing ovals in the moisture left by her glass. "You have to realize how obvious I've been ever since I laid eyes on you that first day, weeks ago, in the cafeteria."

A wrinkle of interest came to his smooth brow. "No, I guess I haven't realized it."

"Well, you hit me like a ton of bricks. I've never been the same since." She raised her eyes solemnly meeting his inquisitive smile. "I haven't been able to eat, sleep, study, or do anything since that day. I growl at my family, bomb out on exams, and am a mess in general." Shaking her head with frustration, she lowered her eyes once more. "And this last week has been the worst. When you didn't call Tuesday like you promised I . . . I just went bananas!"

"Did I promise?" His thick, black brows arched doubtfully.

"You said you would."

"Oh, yes, but did I promise?"

"Well, no, you didn't exactly promise but you told me you'd call me the next day." Karen could feel his annoyance.

"Hey." He put his hands up in mild surrender. "Don't come at me that way." An abrupt scowl shadowed his handsome face.

Karen was momentarily taken back by the sudden change in his mood. This was the first time she had ever seen a frown on the handsome facade. She had to admit that it wasn't flattering. A fleeting thought swept through her mind. It seemed more than a scowl or a hint of anger. It seemed like a warning.

Just as suddenly, a smile emerged on his face. It

was open, bright, and effervescent. She felt foolish for her moment of doubt. "Hey, Karen, if you thought I promised you, then maybe I did give you that impression." He ran his fingers through his tousled curls. "If I did, I'm very sorry." He shrugged his broad shoulders. "It's just that with school, track practice, and then work on my car I didn't have a chance to call."

"It seems as though you could have found a moment to pick up a phone."

"Hey, I think I've already explained that. There's no use going over and over it."

Karen nodded. "You're right. Let's just forget it."

He chucked her playfully beneath the chin. "That's my girl."

She looked up her eyes meeting his. "Am I, Marc?"

He dropped his hand. "Are you what?"

"Am I your girl?"

He looked serious for a moment. "You bet you are."

She shifted about in her seat uncomfortably. "What about Lori then?"

He fidgeted nervously with the edge of his glass. "I only talked to her and sat with her to get back at you."

"Get back at me! What for?"

"You spend a lot of time with that cycle jockey!"

"Do you mean Spike?"

"I don't mean Evil Knievel."

Karen threw her head back and laughed. "I can't

believe this! The whole thing is really very funny."

"To you, maybe."

"It's just that Spike and I grew up together. There's nothing between us other than friendship."

"Yeah, sure. He's got to be far more interested in you than being a person with a ready ear or a shoulder to lean on."

Karen started to tense. "Just what do you mean by that?" Her voice was brittle.

"I saw you out at the track today when you jumped up and put your arms around him. That didn't look like a friendly hug to me."

"I just got excited at one of the events. Neither of us thought a thing about it."

"Then it's not natural, that's all."

Karen closed her eyes for a moment trying to calm down. "Spike is just a friend and that's all he'll ever be. Let's drop it OK?"

"I believe what I see, that's all. I want you to stop seeing him." His voice was low, calculating, cold.

"I . . . I couldn't do that. We practically live next door to each other. He loves to come to my house to see my sister. I can't help running in to him."

Marc leaned forward with a severe intensity. "Maybe we should get something straight right off the start. When I go with a girl she doesn't have any other guys." He jabbed a determined thumb at his chest. "That was the understanding Lisa and I had back in California and that's going to be the understanding here in Riverview."

"I . . . I don't understand."

"You've got to make a choice, that's all. You've got to pick me or the cycle jockey." The intensity of his glare seared into her.

Karen discovered that her back was pressed tightly against the padded back rest. A solid mass had evolved in her throat as she fought back a surge of tears that were pushing up into her eyes. "I'm sorry. I just can't cut Spike out of my life." With disgust, she felt her voice adopting a pitch of desperation. It sounded tenuous, almost shrill. "He's like a brother to me. How could I avoid seeing him?"

Abruptly, he pushed back from the table and started to rise.

"Where . . . where are you going?" Her voice caught with disbelief.

"I'm going home." With a toss of his head which jostled the disarranged, charming tangle of curls, he bolted from the booth on his way to the front door.

Panic flooded through Karen. What had she done? She couldn't allow this to happen—not after all the weeks of pain and longing trying to meet him. Not after last week waiting like a moonstruck calf by the phone that refused to ring. Without a moment of concern as to what others would think, Karen bolted from the booth. She stood, both fists clenched, and shouted for him. "Marc! Come back!" Her voice sounded beseeching. "OK, I won't see him."

Marc stood with his back turned for several moments and at last turned, in an almost military about-face, a huge, wide grin on his face. Karen was puzzled over the expression; it looked almost victorious, almost smug. Slowly, he walked back to the table and stood looking down on her the smile remaining on his lips but his eyes still cold.

Abruptly, he caught her shoulders and pulled her to him and held her. She felt the strength of his arms encircle her and enfold her in his warmth.

Chapter 7

The weight of her school books seemed especially heavy this morning as she trudged up the concrete steps toward the wide, yawning entrance of Central High. It was all she could do to move her feet from one step to the other. Karen knew that she had slept less than four hours the night before. Distastefully, she remembered rolling over with a groan the last time and taking note of the luminous numerals reading 3:20 on the clock on her night stand.

Karen paused at the entrance and sighed before stepping across the threshold. Desperately, she wanted to lay her head down and sleep—sleep for at least twenty-four hours. All night long she had been in a restless self-debate. Should she stop seeing Spike in order to keep Marc? Spike, her lifelong friend, her confidant. Was anyone worth casting aside an old and very reliable friend? Did she place such a pitiful value on her friendship with Spike that she could turn her back on him just because a boy she was infatuated with had given her this ultimatum? Was she that frivolous, that shallow?

Shaking the cobwebs from her mind Karen walked through the door. Immediately the din in the hallways assaulted her senses. Today, she was in no mood for laughter, shouts, and general cutting up. All she wanted, at this moment, was to return to the silence of her bedroom and sleep. All she wanted was to escape for a time.

Slowly, she climbed the steps to the third floor to her locker. It took her three attempts before the tumblers dropped in her combination lock and it opened. Carelessly, she pulled out her geometry book and closed the door. The explosive, metallic sound caused her temple to pulsate.

"Hey, Karen, how ya' doin'?"

Karen looked around and smiled continuing to secure her locker door. "Oh, hi, Sandy," she said without enthusiasm.

"Boy," Sandy said shaking her head, "you look like something the cats dragged in. Those eyes are so blood-shot they look like they should have tourniquets." She giggled placing her arm around Karen's shoulders.

The attempt at humor failed to get the proper response. "Oh," she shrugged, "I suppose I do look a little beat. I didn't sleep very well last night."

"You look like you've been run over by a herd of buffalo."

Karen frowned and turned her head. "Thanks, Sandy. Thanks alot! That's just what I needed."

Sandy pushed her glasses back upon her nose and hunched her shoulders apologetically. "Hey, I'm sorry, Karen. I didn't mean to upset you. I was only trying to get you out of the doldrums." She threw up her hands. "Gee, here the last few days you've looked like the world was coming to an end. From what I hear you should be walking on clouds about now."

Karen looked over to her. "What do you mean?"

"Nothing travels faster than a high school grapevine, you know that. Word is out that the hero of the week is now dating the most popular girl in school." She grinned. "Namely Marc Rodgers and you."

Karen smiled and nodded her head meekly. "Yeah, it's true. Marc and I got together at the Pit Friday after the meet. We talked . . ." She hesitated.

"And . . . and what?" Sandy asked impatiently.

"And I think everything is okay between us now." She looked quickly away avoiding her friend's eyes.

"That's great!" Sandy slapped her on the back. "That's really great! I knew you could do it?" Suddenly, she sobered and a doubtful look emerged upon her face. "Well, if that's the case, why the hound-dog expression on your face? Your chin is practically sweeping the floor."

Karen slumped against her locker. "Oh, I'm really thrilled about Marc and me and everything." She shrugged. "What girl wouldn't? He's tall, handsome, and a hero on the track. He's everything any girl could ever want."

Sandy raised a halting hand. "Wait up. You don't have to convince me. I think he's one of the neatest guys ever to walk the hallowed halls of Central High. I'd say you are a perfect pair."

Karen turned and smiled. "Thanks, Sandy. That's really great of you."

"Yeah, I'm a good kid." She reached back and patted herself on the shoulder. "In fact, I'm one terrific kid."

"You really are, you know that? If I'm ever down in the dumps you're always there to pull me out. I just want you to know that I appreciate it."

"Ah, forget it. You've done the same thing for me plenty of times." She scratched her head. "But, I've got to admit, I'm still confused as to why you feel down and look like the last rose of summer in the first place." She suddenly brightened. "What you need is a good dose of laughter and I know just the person to provide it."

Karen's eyes followed Sandy's gaze down the corridor. Her stomach muscles instantly tightened as she recognized Spike's jaunty, carefree gait.

"Here's Mr. Sunshine himself," Sandy said thrusting out her hand in presentation. "Heeere's . . . Spike!"

Karen looked frantically down the hall in the opposite direction. She searched for any sign of Marc.

Spike approached his mottled face creased in a wide, unassuming grin. His sandy hair was touseled and a rust-colored lock hung boyishly over his forehead almost into his eyes. Raising a hand, he waved enthusiastically.

Karen felt herself being submerged into a warm, protective cocoon of friendship and familiarity. How could she possibly bear to sever the ties of their friendship? She had always depended upon his warmth and advice; he had always been there to give it.

"How's things goin'? Ready to exercise the old cranium once again, guys?"

Karen found herself smiling in spite of herself. She merely nodded her head and looked down the corridor.

"Boy," Spike said with the usual eagerness in his voice, "this kind of weather makes a guy want to get on the old cycle and travel for eternity. The bees are buzzin' and the blossoms are bustin'." He grinned and nudged Sandy with an elbow. "Right, Sandy?"

"Right!" Sandy answered giggling.

"How's about me giving you girls some spins on the bike after school tonight?" He glanced over to Karen but received no response. Finally, he looked over to Sandy. "How about you, Sandy?"

Sandy jumped up clapping her hands; her glasses slid from the bridge to the tip of her nose. She jabbed them back into place. "I'd love it! Would right after school be okay?"

"That would be perfect. I'll pick you up in front of the building about 4:00." He turned back to Karen. "Once I take Sandy home I could come back for you, Karen."

"Oh, no thanks, Spike. I brought the Pumpkin today."

"Maybe some other time, then."

"Right," she said hesitantly, "maybe some other time."

"You'll have all of your transportation problems solved for the rest of the year now, Karen," Sandy offered biting into the corner of her lip mischievously.

"What's that supposed to mean?" Spike's brows furrowed in puzzlement.

"Oh, great news, Spike! Karen and Mark have got it together now and everything is all right." Sandy grinned looking from one to the other.

"That is good news, Karen. It's what you really want, isn't it?"

Karen forced herself to appear ebullient. She smiled bobbing her head eagerly. "Of course it is! I've never been happier in my life. Marc is just great!"

"I'm real happy for you, Karen," Spike said sincerely. Marc seems like a good guy. And I know he's one heck of a runner. That was some performance he put on out there Friday."

"Thanks, Spike. He is a good guy." She avoided his eyes purposely focusing her gaze over his right shoulder. Suddenly, she felt awkward. Abruptly, she shrugged and quickly tapped Sandy on the shoulder. "I've got to get going. I'll see you after school, maybe."

"Maybe the three of us could get a table together at the cafeteria for lunch. I'll save a place for both of you," Spike offered.

"Thanks," Karen said meekly, "but I can't. I get out of Spanish real late sometimes. I wouldn't want to hold you guys up. "She fidgeted nervously with the corner of her book.

"No problem; we'll wait," Spike said.

"No! Don't wait!" The words rushed out too forcefully and she looked down at the floor a flush creeping over her face. Finally, she looked back up into the quizzical expressions. "What I mean is, I might have lunch with Marc or something. I don't know."

Sandy poked her glasses back up upon her nose and smiled. "Hey, that's no problem. That's fine. We'll get together tomorrow or some other time. We know that you and Marc want to be together as much as possible."

Karen had difficulty swallowing. A weak smile barely parted her lips. "Yeah, maybe some other time." She turned and started down the hall to her class. "I'll see you later Sandy. Maybe you could call tonight." With that she walked away.

Sandy looked over to Spike noticing the slight squint of hurt in his eyes. He hunched his shoulders carelessly and motioned for her to accompany him down the opposite corridor.

It was all that Karen could do to contain the tears that were trying to force themselves from the corners of her eyes. Rarely had she ever disliked herself as much as she did right now. She had witnessed the confusion and hurt in Spike's face. How could she have been so blunt, so cold to him? A wave of guilt wafted over her making her almost feel ill. For a moment she closed her eyes feeling a tear escape and trail down her flushed cheek.

"I was hoping I'd run into you before class this morning."

Her heart immediately accelerated at the sound of the low, masculine voice. She looked up into the clear, excited dark-blue eyes and felt her knees growing weak. Consciously, she muffed at her eyes with the side of her hand to prevent him from noticing the tears. "Oh, Marc, hi!" Karen felt his strong hand grip her arm and carefully pull her over to the wall away from the other rushing, bustling students.

"Gee, you look fantastic." He looked down upon her and she wriggled with embarrassment.

She forced herself to smile. "You're either blind or are terribly biased, Marc. I know I don't look my best today. I hardly slept at all last night."

A concerned look crossed his face. "Why? What's the matter? You weren't sick were you?" He placed his hand on her shoulder.

She looked down feeling her throat tighten. "No, not sick. Not sick in the sense you mean it."

"I don't understand. What's that supposed to mean?"

She turned and met his eyes. "It's about what we talked about Friday at the Pit. It's about giving up Spike as a friend."

He dropped his hand and poked it in his side jacket pocket in disgust. "Not that again! I thought we had that all settled. I don't see why we even have to talk about it."

"It's settled as far as you're concerned but it's

still bothering me a lot." She pinched the edge of her lip with her teeth. "I just saw him in the hall a few minutes ago and . . . and I was downright rude to him. I know I must have hurt him."

Marc grinned and hunched his shoulders. "Spike's a big boy, Karen. He'll get over it. If he doesn't get the idea just come out and tell him."

"Come out and tell him! You're talking about someone whom I've been friends with for over ten years!" she said incredulously. A few students talking in the hall turned to look around as her voice increased in pitch and volume. "I could never do that. It's unfair of you to even ask me!"

"Okay, okay, Karen, don't get excited." He gestured with his open hands. "Let him down easy then. Just ignore him and he'll finally get the picture." He shrugged. "Anyway, a guy like Spike has probably got a lot of friends. You can't be presumptuous enough to think that the ending of your relationship would really damage him that much. I'm betting that he doesn't depend upon you that much."

"I know, but . . ."

"He'll get over it. He'll understand. He might even feel the same way if the tables were turned and you were his girl and I was the so-called friend." He squeezed her shoulder. "Don't you see what I mean? Besides, what's important right now is us . . . and only us."

His words caused shivers to race down her back. Karen looked back up into the handsome face, smiled, and nodded her head.

Furtively, he looked up the corridor and then quickly leaned over and placed a quick kiss on her cheek. "I knew you'd see it my way. You're a terrific girl."

Karen smiled but had to admit that she felt far from terrific at the moment.

Marc cupped her chin and raised her eyes to meet his. "Let's just drop the subject. Anyway, I want to talk about what I wanted to see you about before classes started this morning."

"What? I don't understand."

"Well, I think we need to take advantage of a little of this spring sunshine—a spring fling so to speak."

Karen shook her head. "I'm sorry, but you've lost me. I don't have the slightest idea of what you're talking about."

"You will my dear, you will," he said with a wily look on his face as he rubbed his hands together.

Karen burst out in giggles feeling the pall suddenly lift from her shoulders.

"I just think we deserve a little fun this weekend; something different." He pointed to her with an emphatic gesture. "Just you and just me, alone."

Karen liked the sound of it and became instantly intrigued. "What are we going to do? What are your plans?"

He shook his head. "Oh, no, I'm not telling. You won't be able to get it out of me with thumbscrews."

Karen moaned and slapped her forehead. "Oh, can't you at least give me a little hint? I'll go crazy if I have to wait until the weekend."

Poking his tongue beneath his upper lip he looked skyward in deliberation. "I don't know if I should."

"Oh, please, Marc!" Karen squealed. "At least give me a little hint."

He nodded. "I'll just say that I'll be over to your house Saturday after track practice. You will be home won't you?"

"I was thinking of taking the Pumpkin for a drive Saturday afternoon, but that's about all."

"Just don't plan on it, that's all I can say. I'll tell you all of the rest of it when I see you then."

Karen shook her head. "You're going to drive me crazy until Saturday. You do know that don't you?"

"Just bear up until then, beautiful!"

"Oh, you . . . you tyrant!" Karen yelled with mock anger.

The warning bell clanged suddenly interrupting their conversation.

"We'd better get going," Marc warned. "I'll try to call you sometime tonight. Okay?"

"Okay. That would be nice."

"See ya' later, then." Abruptly, he gave her a strong hug and turned to hurry down the hall.

Karen watched him leave feeling warm and good but yet torn with emotion concerning Spike.

Chapter 8

Karen had just closed the door in anticipation of Marc's arrival. She turned her head as she heard a loud, sonorous blast as the maroon Camaro rode up to the curb. Her heart quickened as she saw Marc's handsome head poke through the side window, wave and beckon to her.

Her chest constricted with emotion as she gazed at his handsome, smiling face. He wrenched the door open and she hopped in beside him.

"Thanks for picking me up. I think it's about time I gave the Pumpkin a rest. Its brakes are really sounding bad."

"No trouble," he said with a wink and gathered her close to him. "I am always at your service." He put the car into gear and screeched away from the curb.

Karen sighed and sat back in the seat closing her eyes. "Oh, it's a beautiful spring afternoon. I came out of the house and took a deep breath and nearly floated right off of my feet."

"You can't give spring all the credit for that," he quipped slyly.

She looked over to him and smiled. "I know that. I really feel wonderful! You make me feel that way when I'm with you."

"Those are my exact words when I'm with you, babe." He gave her a slight, affectionate tug and pulled her closer.

"Oh, Marc, I just hate to think about spending the rest of the term sitting in a musty old classroom cooped up all day away from the beautiful sunshine. The only thing I can think of is getting outside into the fresh air."

"I feel the same way. It's almost a crime to make us sit there forcing ourselves to study when we could be doing a whole lot of other neat things."

She sighed again and stretched. "I know, but there's not a thing we can do about it. We're just teenagers, you know. Anyway, since it's Saturday let's just enjoy the day and worry about school on Monday. She sighed. "Now will you tell me what you were so mysterious about in school the other day? I've been at my wits end all week."

Marc motioned with his head. "Take a look in the back seat."

Karen twisted around and looked at two grocery bags setting on the seat. "What . . . ?"

"In those brown bags, my fair lady, you will find a cornucopia of edible delights." His dark-blue eyes rolled upwards in reflection. "Hot dogs, potato chips, black seedless olives, pork and beans, Cokes, and sardines in mustard sauce."

"Sardines in mustard sauce! Yech!"

"Yes, sardines in mustard sauce. They are my

weakness . . . my passion." He held a hand dramatically to his chest. "I love them almost . . . almost as much as I do you."

Karen started to laugh but sobered as the impact of his last statement struck her. "Will you be serious? What is all of this for?"

"A picnic, my fair lady." He took a deep breath. "I decided when I got up this morning that today was too beautiful to be anywhere but outdoors. It is a day when all free souls should be free. So after track practice I cruised over to the quick shop and picked up a few things."

"Sounds wonderful! Do you suppose we could find a spot where there's a stream?" Karen asked.

He reached over and gave her a warm hug. "Sure. I know just the spot. I found it right after we moved here."

Karen smiled and snuggled close to him. She felt giddy with happiness.

Karen lay back, her hands clasped behind her head, allowing the sun that filtered through the towering pines to sprinkle onto her face. She breathed deep, inhaling the multiple scents of the evergreens, wild mountain flowers, and the forest. With one eye, she squinted to look up at Marc diligently working with a pocket knife, trying to open the can of sardines. She felt good; she felt free.

Suddenly her nose twitched and she opened her eyes to look up at a sardine dangling precariously above her.

"Come on, I want you to try one. They're delicious," he pleaded.

Karen shook her head vigorously. "No! You can't make me. I'd rather die first."

Mark pulled the little fish away from her and popped it into his mouth. He sat there like a contented cat running his tongue over his upper lip. "You don't know what you're missing."

She grimaced making a face. "I'll just have to suffer, I guess."

A mischievous glint came to his eyes and Karen sat up immediately noticing the change. "What are you planning to do?" She scooted back from him. "I don't like the way you're looking at me."

Marc dug his fingers into the can and pulled out another mustard-coated fish. "I just will not give up until you experience this gourmet delight." He got to his feet and started toward her.

Expectantly, with a look of dread on her face, Karen rose to her feet as well. "Marc, I'm warning you . . ."

He bolted forward and she shrieked parrying away with him. With a solid thud he fell flat onto his face but still held tenaciously to the little fish.

Karen took advantage of his fall to race to a pine tree. Breathlessly, she hid behind it. Peeking out, she saw him get to his feet once again, his eyes searching for her.

"Come on out, Karen," he teased. "Come on out and take your medicine." He held the sardine daintily by the tail with two fingers.

Karen pressed her fist to her mouth trying to stifle her giggles.

He came close enough to her to touch. She screamed and darted away. He came running in pursuit through weeds, fallen pine cones, and bright breathtaking bouquets of wild flowers.

Karen ran laughing uncontrollably, feeling his presence dangerously close.

Her breathing was belabored and a glance over her shoulder told her he was but a few yards behind. Suddenly, her foot hit a root and she fell, in a sprawl of arms and legs, to the ground. Marc was at her side immediately dangling the little fish over her mouth.

She giggled uproariously and as she did he released the fish. Instantly, she bolted upright, her eyes protruding, clutching at her throat. "I . . . I swallowed it!" she gasped.

A pleased expression flooded over Marc's face. "Good, wasn't it?"

"I . . . I really don't know. I swallowed it whole without really tasting it."

Marc threw his head back convulsing with laughter, finally crumpling to the ground. He lay there laughing hysterically until he clutched his sides. His happy, open laughter was contagious and soon Karen found herself joining him.

"That . . . that expression on your face was something else when that fish went down your throat."

"It really wasn't so bad going down that fast," she giggled.

Marc sat up and looked at her. "You're a terrific sport, Karen." He pulled a handkerchief from his back pocket and wiped away the mustard at the corner of her mouth. For a moment their eyes fused and Karen tensed as he started to lean forward.

"I . . . I think we'd better get back to the picnic. I think I'd like another hot dog before the fire goes out."

"Sure," he said with a smile. He reached down and carefully tugged her to her feet.

Karen felt warm and tingly as his arm encircled her shoulders walking back to camp.

They spent the rest of the day taking walks along mountain trails, picking wild flowers, wading in the icy streams, and talking. Karen could never remember a more beautiful day. It was everything she had always dreamed of.

And then as the chill of evening suddenly came upon them Marc relit the camp fire and placed his sweater snugly around her shoulders. They sat there together watching the fire.

"Are you glad you came, Karen?"

She looked up into his eyes seeing the reflection of the flames in them. "Oh, yes. Today has been wonderful!"

"You've been wonderful, Karen."

She looked shyly away. Suddenly, she felt his hand cup her chin and pull her around to him. He tilted her head so he was looking directly down into her eyes. "You know, Karen, you're really something."

Her heart raced out of control as she watched his head lean forward and felt the warmth of his lips meet hers. For a moment she felt dizzy with ecstasy. She wanted this moment to last forever.

Chapter 9

Sandy nudged her glasses back upon her nose as she craned her neck forward to catch Karen's every word about her date with Marc. "Gee," she said slapping her hand over her mouth, "weren't your parents ticked off at you getting in so late? My parents would've grounded me until Christmas."

Karen shook her head solemnly. "Luckily, they weren't home. I feel real guilty about the whole thing now." She shrugged and looked up the busy corridor.

"What's that supposed to mean? You look like you've lost your best friend instead of finally trapping the neatest guy in school."

Karen turned to her. "Sandy, I don't know. I'm really confused. I feel like I'm being pulled apart like a wishbone. In the first place, I'm thrilled at being with Marc. He's everything a girl could want. And he does have the neatest set of wheels in school."

"So? I'm sorry, but you're not going to get much pity from me. I think you've about got everything now."

Karen winced. "I know it looks that way and I am excited about going with him but . . ."

"But what?" Sandy asked staring into Karen's eyes.

"Marc doesn't want me to see Spike again."

"Why not?" Sandy asked with disbelief.

"He thinks there's something between us other than being just very good friends."

Sandy placed her hands on hips staunchly. "Do you mean he ordered you to stop seeing Spike?"

Karen looked away. "That's just about the size of it."

Sandy huffed indignantly. "Well, I'd just tell him to go soak his head."

Karen was about to reply, to explain, when she felt a finger prod her back.

"Am I breaking something up?"

Karen instantly sobered as she turned and looked up into Marc's deep blue eyes. He grinned, exhibiting his flawless, white teeth.

Oh, hi," Karen said strangely feeling herself tense.

"Hey, listen, babe I've got to talk to you."

Karen looked at him and then back to Sandy who was standing patiently, her arms wrapped abound her books. "Did you see Sandy standing here with me, Marc?"

He smiled. "Oh, sure. Hi, Sandy. What's happening?"

Sandy smiled and started to reply but Marc abruptly turned his back to her. Instinctively, she backed away, a bit hurt at the rebuff.

"Hey, right after school a few of us are running

over to Pineview to see what's going on. How about coming with us?"

"Pineview? That's forty miles away. Besides, I've got cheerleading practice and you've got track."

"Big deal!" he said waving his hand. "I'm skipping practice. Coach Gordon will understand."

"But I've got to go to cheerleading practice," Karen protested. "One more unexcused absence and I could get kicked off the squad."

"No sweat. I've seen you cheerlead and you don't need any practice. You're perfect just the way you are."

"I . . . I just can't. Besides, my folks don't want me going that far out of town after school."

He shook his head sullenly. "Oh no, not one of those goody-goodies. What do you want to do, tell them everything you do? Hey, you've got lots to learn. In this war its parents versus teenagers. You've got to use every tactic, every strategy, in every battle."

Karen looked up at him quizzically. "My parents and I have always been open with each other. We always talk over our problems. It's worked out fine up until now."

"Yeah, but now comes the time when all of that goes down the drain. When you're old enough to want a little fun or a little independence they'll put the clamps down on you." He jabbed a thumb at his chest. "I've been that route and I know from experience."

"May I say something?" Sandy stuck her head over Karen's shoulder.

"No, butt out! This is between Karen and me.

Don't you have a class to go to or something?" He glanced over to Sandy with a look of anger on his face.

A crimson flush came to Sandy's face. "I only was going to . . ."

Marc threw up his hands in disgust. "No, man, I've had it! I'm not standing around here to get ganged up on by two females. "If you don't want to go to Pineview with me, that's fine." He started away. Suddenly, he stopped and looked over his shoulder. "You and your friend have a good time swigging Cokes at the Pit while the rest of us are enjoying ourselves at Pineview." He grinned cynically, tossed his head, and waved his hand, carelessly continuing down the hall.

Karen choked back the tears as she watched him walk jauntily down the corridor.

"That's not the same person who met you at the Pit, is it?" Sandy asked disbelievingly. "He was so nice there. This person is entirely different. It's like Jekyll and Hyde."

Pressing her fist beneath her nose, Karen could feel the tears surface in her eyes. "I . . . I don't know what to do."

"You can't go, of course. Your parents would have a fit if you went that far out of town."

"Yes, but if I don't go, I'll lose him. He'll probably go with Lori." She shook her head. A smooth, silken lock of hair tumbled down over her forehead; with a swoop of her hand she threw it back into place. "Do you see what I mean when I said I feel like a wishbone?"

"Yes, I sure do," Sandy answered thoughtfully.

The two girls stood with their backs resting against their lockers, neither speaking as they watched Lori Mobley approach on her way to class. Their eyes followed her shifting, sensuous gait as she passed. Karen winced as she absorbed the enticing full figure encased in a skin-tight pair of jeans and sweater.

"How many minutes before the bell?" Karen asked distractedly.

Sandy checked her watch. "Just a couple. Why?"

Karen turned and started to jog down the hall. "Because I'm going to tell Marc that I'm going with him to Pineview after school. If my folks call you, don't say anything!"

Before Sandy could answer Karen had disappeared around the turn in the hall. Sandy turned dejectedly to walk to her own class. A strange bolt of anger suddenly plummeted through her. Abruptly, she swung her head from one side and then another to peer down the vacant hall and then slammed her foot against the door of a locker. She grimaced at the pain in her great toe. The loud metallic crash made an echo in the empty hall.

Chapter 10

Karen lifted the receiver at the first jingle. She wanted to be sure that the sound didn't disturb the rest of the sleeping family. She spoke into it in a low, stealthy voice. "Hello?"

"Sorry to call so late, Karen. But, I was just about to bust my buttons to find out what happened up at Pineview."

Karen instantly recognized Sandy's familiar voice. "We had a lot of fun . . . I guess."

"You guess. What do you mean by that? You either had fun or you didn't, that's all there is to it."

Karen sighed and lay back her arm cradling her head. "I wish life was all that simple."

"Are you getting philosophical with me, Karen Marie Cooper? Don't get heavy with all of this."

Karen laughed cautiously. "I know it sounds crazy but that's how I feel. I did have fun but at the same time I felt terribly guilty for missing cheerleading practice again and being so far out of town. I've got three unexcused absences. And I know my parents wouldn't approve of my being that far out of town and especially at Pineview."

"What did your parents say to you when you got home?"

"Luckily my dad had a meeting and my mom and Dody were at Mrs. Percell's discussing the Church Bazaar." A deep sigh sifted between her teeth. "I know I wasn't home ten minutes when they all came in."

"You must have been born under the right sign, girl. How could anyone be so lucky?"

"Yeah," Karen nodded, "I agree."

"Well?" Sandy inquired.

"Well, what?" Karen returned.

Sandy gasped in exasperation. "Who was there and what did you do? I know this: Pineview is way up in the mountains and has some very tricky roads."

"Lori, Mick Fredericks, Marc and I were the only ones in the car."

"Mick Fredericks!" Sandy exclaimed in disbelief. "Karen, you know that that guy is strictly bad news. He's been suspended from school more times than I can count."

"I know. When I saw him and Lori sitting in the backseat of Marc's car I about did an about-face and left."

"Why did Marc have them along anyway? He doesn't usually run around with Mick Fredericks."

"I guess it's because Mick is interested in Marc's car. He's sort of a racing fanatic or something. Marc wanted to show him how fast he could take the Pineview Road."

"That sounds scary, Karen!" Sandy shrieked.

"Believe me, it was. I was on the edge of my seat the entire descent."

"Your folks would have had a fit if they knew you were taking such chances."

"I know. I have to admit that I was genuinely scared out of my wits."

"Marc shouldn't have taken risks like that with other people in the car. Those hairpin curves are treacherous."

"He claimed that he was in perfect control at all times."

"Famous last words."

"There was a time or two that I felt there could have been a disaster. I guess I just don't have the adventure in me that most people have."

"You've just got more common sense, that's all. That could have been curtains for all of you. There are places up there that drop two miles into canyons."

"I know. I was looking into those canyons all the way down the road."

"How did Lori react?"

Karen smiled to herself in revery. "Most of the time she was chewing her gum furiously, squealing, or just crouching down into the seat, her eyes buried in her hands."

Sandy giggled on the other end. "I really can't say I blame her."

"Of course, I'm a good one to talk," Karen admitted, "I was sitting so rigid I'm sure they all thought I had become instantly petrified."

"At least you're laughing, Karen. That's a good

sign. I thought the other day at school you seemed really down. I couldn't quite pinpoint it but I thought you seemed sort of ill at ease around Spike."

"Did he say anything to you after I left?"

"No. You know Spike; he would never complain or anything."

Karen sighed and fluffed her pillow impatiently. "I might as well admit everything to you, Sandy." A tension-filled pause took over for several moments.

"Go on. What is it? Don't keep me in suspense."

Begrudgingly, Karen continued. "Well, it's like I started to tell you earlier today. Marc doesn't want me to have anything to do with Spike any more."

"What do you mean? I don't think I understand."

"Well, it's pretty simple. He just doesn't want me to be friends with him."

"What! Why not?" Sandy gasped.

"I don't know. It's just a thing with him. It has something to do with his ego, I suppose."

"It sounds to me like he's an egomaniac. I hope you set him straight. You never had time to tell me today."

A longer pause ensued.

"Karen?" Sandy asked. "You did tell Marc to forget it, didn't you?"

"No. I'm afraid I didn't." Karen's voice came through in an anemic whisper.

"Do you mean to tell me that you're going to break off a ten-year friendship with Spike?" she asked incredulously.

"Marc just doesn't understand. He doesn't think that a girl can have a boyfriend as well as a boy who is a friend at the same time. He wouldn't permit it with his last relationship in California and he won't permit it with me."

"Permit! Did you say, permit? I can't believe that I'm talking to Karen Cooper—Miss Independence. Since when do you let a boy dictate to you like that?"

Karen could feel herself tense and a sudden surge of anger goad at her. "He's not dictating to me, Sandy!"

"Oh," Sandy said casually. "I guess that means that you're not going to do what he wants you to do. Right?"

Karen refused to answer for a moment.

"Right, Karen?"

"No. It means that I'm going to stop seeing Spike if it will please Marc."

"I can't believe what I'm hearing!"

"I'm sorry, Sandy, but I've made up my mind. You don't seem to understand what Marc means to me."

"I just know this: you've known Marc just a few weeks whereas you've known Spike for ten years. I'm not saying I want you to end it with Marc but don't you think you owe Spike something?"

"Of course I owe Spike something. He's a very good and valued friend. He's helped me out more times than I can count over the years. I'm . . ." Her voice broke briefly. ". . . I'm going to be lost without him."

"Well, then, forget this Marc Rodgers and return to the land of the living. That guy is existing in another century."

"I can't do that, Sandy. I've already promised Marc that I would break off my friendship with Spike."

"It's just not fair."

"Things aren't always fair, Sandy. You know that."

"Yeah, but this is wrong. This just shouldn't happen to a great guy like Spike. Gee, this will really hurt him. I could see it myself, in his eyes, when you treated him so coldly in the hall the other day."

A jolt of wrenching frustration shot through Karen. She bit into her lower lip mercilessly. "Sandy, don't judge me. You're my friend. You're supposed to be giving me some help, some assurance."

"I'm sorry, Karen. I can't."

"What do you mean?"

"I mean exactly that. I can't pat you on the back and say you're doing the right thing. Not in this case; that would be hypocritical. I think you're trading a beautiful friendship for an unstable relationship at best."

"Don't start with your philosophies on life again!" Karen snapped. "Don't you think I've got enough self-doubt now?"

Sandy's voice suddenly acquired an unusual abrasiveness. "No, Karen. I'm not just going to mimic words that you want to hear like a parrot or something. I think what you are doing is totally wrong and I won't go along with it."

Karen sighed and closed her eyes briefly to collect her senses. Rarely, did Sandy and she disagree. "I . . . I just thought maybe I could get a little support from you, that's all. After all, you are my best friend."

"And what does that mean, Karen? If Marc wants you to break off your friendship with me, would you do it? He seems to be able to control you pretty well."

"That's not fair! It's not the same thing and you know it. I would never do anything to damage our relationship."

"I don't see that it's any different than the friendship you and Spike have."

"The point is that Marc thinks there is a definite difference."

"If he'd only come down off his pedestal he could see that there is no difference."

"You just don't understand. I'm just not taking any chances of losing Marc. If you could have only seen the way he was on our picnic in the mountains last weekend you'd think differently of him."

"Oh, I know he's good looking and he drives that great set of wheels. He's even charming when his ego is getting fed and he gets his way. But, I've also seen him when he thought that he wasn't getting his way. It wasn't a very pretty sight. He can be pretty juvenile and rude during those times."

"Well, I've made up my mind and that's that. I want Marc and if I have to make sacrifices to get him, I will."

"And this includes sacrificing long-standing friendships, huh, Karen?" Sandy's voice acquired a tone of sadness.

Suddenly Karen could feel a weariness envelope her. The receiver seemed to have gained extra weight in her hand. She had always loved to talk to Sandy on the phone by the hour but tonight she just wanted to end the conversation and to go to sleep. "I don't think we're getting anywhere here, Sandy. I'm tired and it's getting late. Maybe we could continue this some other time."

"What's to continue?" Sandy asked cynically, "You've already made up your mind. I just hope you can sleep with a decision like that."

Anger prickled at Karen's scalp. "I'll sleep just fine, Sandy. Don't you worry. And thanks a lot for all of your support!"

"I can't give it when I don't feel it, Karen."

Karen sighed. "Well, that's been gone over before. I'll talk to you again some other time when we're both more clearheaded."

"I don't think I'm the one you're talking about."

Karen gripped the receiver until her knuckles became pale. "See you later, Sandy. Good night."

Karen allowed the receiver to drop with an abrupt emphasis back onto the hook displaying her disappointment and anger.

Reaching over, Karen switched off the lamp on her night stand. Raising her head she pummeled her pillow viciously venting her anger. With a huge exhalation of breath she fell onto it and stared up into the blackness of her room. Questions raced and collided in her muddled brain as before. Answers seemed to sneak shyly into focus and were accepted because they were to her liking or were convenient. She squirmed about with discomfort.

Karen tossed about in her bed trying one position and then another. Was this going to be another sleepless night bombarded with questions and devoid of answers? Was she really terrible for accepting Marc's ultimatum about losing him if she didn't end her friendship with Spike? Did this expose a flaw, a shallowness in her character?

She lay there mentally comparing the two boys. Spike was a happy-go-lucky person. He cared about people. She could still see him rolling around on the floor wrestling playfully with Dody. He had always been kind and considerate to Dody without ever showing her a moment of pity. Spike had always brought the best out in her. What would happen to Spike and Dody's relationship if she broke off their friendship? Dody needed his attention, his caring, and his love.

And what about the many times in the past when she, herself, had a problem or just needed someone to talk to? Wasn't Spike always there giving his time and attention. Maybe, he never had all of the answers but she always felt better after talking to him. What about all of the years that they had invested in their friendship—all of the good times and the bad? Didn't that count for anything? A friendship like their's may just come along once or twice in a lifetime. Was she willing to give all of that up?

But then there was Marc. Never in her life had she met a boy more handsome, more dynamic, more charming, than Marc. When he smiled she could feel herself wilt in surrender. On the track he was poetry in motion: strong, muscular, and graceful. Everyone in school was in awe over him. The guys yearned for his athletic ability and the girls were envious of her relationship with him. But yet he was a paradox. He had so much going for him: talent, charm, good looks. And yet, it seemed that he needed people to feed or bolster his ego as though he were totally unsure of himself. Karen thought back to the Pit that day after the track meet where he went from table to table collecting praise and accolades. Spike would have never needed that. He was much more self-assured, more mature.

Karen recalled the treacherous run down Pineview Road and the terror which had swept over her as they squealed with smoking tires around the hairpin curves. He had to prove to everyone that he was the very best driver of all. He wouldn't be satisfied until he had a time that no one else could compare to. Marc needed to feed that self-indulged beast—his ego. He needed to salve his fragile self-pride. Karen winced at the recollection.

But there were other times, good times. Karen lay there and smiled up into the darkness. There was that wonderful day on the picnic in the mountains. Marc had been different there, more genuine, more relaxed. He didn't have to prove anything to anyone that day out there with her. Karen chuckled to herself as she recalled how he had laughed at her reaction as he dropped the mustard sardine into her mouth. She smiled contentedly as she remembered him chasing her through the radiant groves of mountain flowers. With warm fondness she recalled their walks together on the trails, their icy barefoot treks into the streams. She remembered his concern as he placed his sweater about her shoulders as they sat next to the crackling fire watching the flames lick and leap upward into the night. Karen remembered how he held her and the warmth and tenderness of his kiss.

Suddenly, confusion and hurt plummeted through her and she felt herself shudder beneath its pressure. Abruptly, she placed the edge of her blanket between her teeth to stifle her sobs.

Chapter 11

The next day Karen sat staring at her jagged thumbnail. Reaching for her purse, she took out a file and smoothed its edge. Her pulse was still racing as she recalled the loud, booming announcement over the intercom that she was wanted in Dr. Melford's office immediately. Throughout her years at Central High she had heard, numerous times, names summoned over the intercom. It caused lifted brows for it usually meant that someone had transgressed again. She recalled how the eyes swung in her direction during geometry class. She was sure her face had blushed to crimson. Mrs. Broderick had nodded silently indicating that she was excused to leave at once.

The thick padded leather chair made a sound resembling a saddle as she shifted uneasily. Now and then she looked up to catch Margie's furtive, questioning glances. She and Margie used to quip and joke together when she would come to the office on an errand or something, but this was entirely different.

Karen tried her best to look controlled even though she could feel the tumult going on at the pit of her stomach. With frustration, she tossed the file back into her purse. It had to be about a combination of things: her grades, unexcused absences at cheerleading practice. She shook her head and rubbed her temple trying to clear out the cobwebs in her brain. Too many things had happened too fast.

Karen lurched as Dr. Melford's office door swung open and he appeared looking more somber, more foreboding than she could ever remember. His gray brows ran along a bushy row above his eyes in a scowl. Margie looked around from her typewriter with an expression of sympathy on her face.

"Karen Cooper, please come in." His voice remained deep and even, giving no indication of his temperament.

Karen rose to her feet smoothing her skirt. She tried her best to look casual even though she could feel herself start to tremble.

He walked into his office, closed the door, and gestured for her to take a seat immediately across from him. She imagined that there had been countless victims in the past occupying this same chair. Mentally, she could see them squirming in anguish.

Dr. Melford cleared his throat and grimaced as though he had tasted something bitter. He looked up with a piercing gaze and Karen lowered her head.

"Karen, I called you in here today to clear up a

few matters that have been bothering the faculty, your teachers, of late." Pursing his lips, clasping his hands at his chest, he contemplated on how to continue. "The three years you have been here at Central High have been good, productive years for you. You have been an exemplary student and have always represented what was good at Central High."

Raising her head, Karen met his keen, intelligent dark eyes.

"I have received several reports in the past two months that have caused me some concern." He cleared his throat once again and laced his fingers atop his glass-covered desk. "Three of your instructors have voiced concern with your rapidly falling grades." He paused, waiting for her to reply. When it was apparent that she would not, he continued. "I realize that this sometimes happens to active, extroverted young people like yourself. Things mount up, pressures come upon you." He looked toward the ceiling in reflection. "Many of us adults do not even come close to realizing the stress and pressures that you young people are under these days. Even teachers and administrators, whose job it is to understand young people, do not know." Subconsciously, he ran a finger beneath his starched collar. "Sometimes, I think I lose contact with reality and the students up here in my ivory tower, only coming in contact with them when some disciplinary measures must be taken. In other words, I only view the bad things. I do know that young people today are mostly made up of fine, intelligent, positive individuals."

Karen involuntarily stiffened in her chair. Here it comes, she thought.

"Many times, I wish I were back in the classroom teaching science." Again, he looked toward the ceiling. "Those were my best days." Abruptly, he shrugged and looked back at her. "What I am trying to relate, in my roundabout fumbling way, is my concern for a student who was doing so well in all phases of her school life, academic and social, and who suddenly is losing ground so fast that it is frightening." He looked to her once again anticipating a reply. "Would you like to say anything at this time?"

Karen stared at the floor and shook her head.

"I assured myself that your falling grades were only temporary and you would soon bring them up once again. I resolved to do or say nothing for another week." He smoothed his thick brows with a sweep of his palm. "That is, until Miss Lathrop came in this morning and informed me that you would no longer be a member of the varsity cheerleading squad due to three unexcused absences."

Looking up, Karen winced at the finality of his words.

"This saddened me greatly. I think you were a grand participant on that squad. No one had more school spirit, enthusiasm, and talent, I might add, than you."

Karen looked up into Dr. Melford's eyes and suddenly saw something other than a school administrator, remote and cold. She saw a man who genuinely liked young people, who wanted to help them. She saw a man who did have to be firm at times to control student behavior but also who was hurt when a student he particularly had great hopes for failed. In a way it meant that he and the school had failed as well. Suddenly, she saw him as someone's grandfather, kind and understanding.

"Miss Lathrop and I thought perhaps I should talk to you. This sudden academic malfunctioning, I suppose we could call it, and your unexcused absences at cheerleading practice, indicated to us that something was amiss." His voice grew soft, almost beseeching. "Karen, if there is anything I or any of us can possibly do to get you back on the track, just tell us. You are too fine a young lady to allow all of this to happen to you."

Karen looked him evenly in the eyes and spoke. She surprised even herself at how strong and confident her voice sounded. "There's nothing anyone can do. I have no excuse for not going to practice and Miss Lathrop has every right to drop me from the squad. As far as my grades, I will try harder. I guess maybe I've been kind of lax with studying lately. I'll try harder from now on."

"Perhaps, a talk with Mr. Wilder, our counselor."

"No, that won't be necessary. I'll be fine now."

Dr. Melford nodded halfheartedly, still unconvinced that anything had been thoroughly settled. Suddenly, as if a dial had been turned, his firm, business-like manner and voice returned. "I have to warn you that if another teacher reports to me about you a call to your parents will be in order. Do you understand this?"

Karen nodded. "Yes, I understand."

A pause settled in between them. He seemed to be waiting to allow her every opportunity to seek help. Finally, he cleared his throat, got up out of his swivel chair, walked to the door and opened it. "You may go now. I hope this little talk has helped in some small way."

Karen got to her feet and looked up at him at the threshold. "It has, Dr. Melford. Believe me, it has." With that she went through the door ignoring Margie's interested stare as she left the outer office.

As she closed the door, she stood against it a few moments trying to calm the sick feeling swirling in her stomach. Pressing her books to her chest, she bit into her lower lip to keep from breaking into tears.

"I couldn't believe it when I heard your name announced over the intercom first period."

Karen had been so absorbed that she failed to see Sandy standing at the door of the principal's office waiting for her.

"Oh, hi, Sandy," she tried hard to sound casual, uncaring.

"Hi, Sandy! Is that all you've got to say?" Sandy slapped the side of her face and nudged the thick glasses back on to her nose. "You get a call into the Fox's office and all you've got to say is . . ."

"Oh, stop being so melodramatic!" Karen's

voice reeked with anger as she rudely brushed by her friend.

Sandy stood there a moment watching Karen walk quickly away. "Hey, wait!" she called running up behind her. "What is this?" Grabbing Karen's shoulder, she brought her to a halt. "Don't you recognize me? I'm Sandy Benjamin your confidant and best friend for the last five years. I'm the girl who has been with you through all of your crises from your first pimple to choosing your first training bra." She paused and winced as she realized she had failed to evoke any laughter from her.

"I . . . I'm sorry. I just have to get to my next class." Karen looked away from her inquisitive eyes.

Sandy's voice lowered and became soft. "Hey, we share everything, remember? Remember when I told you I had a secret crush on Liz Hawkin's dad? Of course, the fact that he sold wholesale candy didn't have any influence on me." She grinned looking into Karen's solemn face. "And remember when you told me that you were planning to run away from home and become a famous ballerina? Also, the fact that you never had a lesson in your life didn't seem to matter."

"I really should get to class, Sandy," Karen said looking down the hall.

Sandy hit her friend lightly on the shoulder. "Hey, I'm just here to help, that's all. I know if I was going under for the third and last time I'd want someone to throw me a life preserver."

Karen turned to her, her eyes flashing with sudden anger. "I'm not going under for the third and last time! I'm fine! Why is everyone suddenly so concerned about Karen Cooper?" She gestured, jutting out her palms. "I am the same girl I was a few months ago. I haven't changed! I'm just having a little difficulty concentrating on school right now, that's all. I just want all of the so-called concerned people to butt out! If I want their help, I'll ask for it!" Brusquely, she turned away and hurried down the hall.

Sandy stood there, her mouth gaping open in bewilderment. She had failed to see the tears of hurt streaming down her best friend's face.

Karen pulled the Pumpkin into the drive with a screech of the unoiled brakes. Slamming the door, she tucked her books beneath her arm and made her way across the neatly clipped front lawn toward her house. A lassitude had enveloped her the latter part of the day and the only thing that had been in her mind since the fourth period was to get home and get to her room and lie down. She could feel the stares and overhear the whispers of other students as she walked down the hall between classes. Everyone was curious as to what had happened to Karen Cooper. She felt that she should have been wearing some sort of tag around her neck denoting that she was a criminal or something.

Just as she reached for the knob on the door, she looked towards Spike's house. Karen noticed a

pair of long, gangly legs encased in dirty jeans ending with huge feet fitted into a pair of ragged,
soiled sneakers sticking out from beneath a motorcycle. A pang of nostalgia wafted through her for a
moment. She needed to talk to someone; someone
who understood. Spike was always there when she
needed him. Marc's words echoed in her head. Biting into her lower lip, she made up her mind.
Laying her books on the porch, she walked slowly
over to him.

"Hand me that rachet wrench there in the box,
would you?" Spike asked lying beneath the cycle.

"I don't know a rachet wrench from a screw-
driver." She held up various tools until he nodded
his approval.

"Brakes needed adjusting," he muttered, continuing to work. "Just about collided with a city bus
an hour ago."

"Nothing happened did it? I mean you didn't actually hit it or anything did you?" She was surprised at the urgency in her voice.

"Naw," he waved a grease-coated hand. "I
missed it by a mile but for a minute I thought my
heart was going to exit via my throat."

Karen smiled in spite of herself.

"Sounds to me as if the Pumpkin's brakes could
use a little work, also."

"Yes, I've noticed that every time I press down
on the brake pedal they squeal."

"Probably needs a little brake fluid. I'll check it
later."

"Thanks, I'd really appreciate it." She stood and

watched his dirty fingers deftly work on the machine. "I guess you're wondering why I'm home so early, huh?"

"Never gave it a thought."

"I mean, I'm usually a lot later than this since I have cheerleading practice."

Spike glanced at his watch and nodded. "Yeah, I guess you're right. You are home early."

She licked her dry lips. "I . . . I got dropped from the squad today."

He looked out from beneath the cycle, a streak of grease running across his freckled face. "Gee, I'm sorry, Karen."

She shrugged carelessly trying to smile. "Oh, I'll survive. It's not the end of the world."

"I know that, but you were the best one on the squad. It won't be the same without you."

"Thanks for saying that. I really mean it. Thanks a lot."

"Don't mention it; it's how I feel." Self-consciously, he adjusted his baseball cap and returned to work.

"Aren't you going to ask me why I was dropped?"

"I just supposed if you wanted me to know you would tell me."

A solid lump quickly materialized in Karen's throat and she struggled to speak. "You're pretty special, do you know that, Spike?"

His pale-blue, nondescript eyes looked up from under the bill of his cap and he smiled. "You're pretty special too, Karen."

Karen looked away as she felt the tears ebb from the corners of her eyes and run, in tiny rivulets, down her cheeks.

Spike noticed and was up on his feet and at her side in a moment. "Hey, Karen, what did I say?" He shook his head with concern. "If I said anything I shouldn't have, I'm real sorry. You know how clumsy I am with words."

With bleary, tear-streaked eyes, she looked up into the solemn, speckled face. "No, you said just the right thing; that's why I'm blubbering this way."

Raising his hands high into the air he allowed them to free-fall with a slap to his sides. "I guess I'll never understand women!" Pulling a handkerchief from his back pocket, he handed it to Karen.

With a swipe she wiped the tears from her face and dabbed at her eyes. "Just stay the way you are; never change." She brought her hand up and worked at a grease smudge on his cheek.

He stood there waiting until she had finished. He licked his lips nervously. "Karen, does all this have anything to do with the jock?"

"Do you mean Marc?"

He nodded.

Karen looked away and nodded. "Yes, I suppose it does. But, a lot of it is my own fault." She cocked her head in thought for a moment. "How did you know anyway?"

"Sandy phoned me yesterday."

"I should have known," she said disgustedly.

Spike held up his hand in front of her face. "Now, wait a minute. Sandy is a good friend; she's worried about you."

Karen avoided his inquiring eyes.

"She said that you just weren't acting like yourself lately."

"She didn't have to tell me, I noticed it too."

Karen shrugged and looked away. "I am the same. Things have just been going wrong, that's all."

"Tell me about it."

"Why should I? Didn't Sandy fill you in?"

"I want to hear it from you."

She closed her eyes for a moment and sighed. "Well, my grades are rock bottom lately. I've missed cheerleading practice three times without a legitimate excuse. I haven't been getting along with my parents very well. I was very rude to one of my best friends." She tried to smile. "How's that for an all-around mess of things?"

"Anything else?"

She sighed deeply. "Well, I might as well tell you, Marc does not want me to see you any more."

His face remained expressionless. "I see. And what do you want?"

Karen pressed Spike's arm. "You don't even have to ask that. We've been the best of friends for ten years. I tried to tell him that." She looked away dejectedly. "I might as well have talked to a brick wall."

"I guess he just doesn't understand."

"That's the understatement of the year. He

doesn't think any girl and boy can just be friends. He's convinced that there's always more to it than that." She shook her head in exasperation. "He's . . . so . . . so narrowminded!"

"He sounds a little insecure to me, Karen."

Looking away, she shook her head. "I don't know; I just don't know."

"So what are you going to do?"

Turning, she met his eyes. "I don't know. I promised him I would stop seeing you, but that's silly."

"It looks like you've already broken your promise."

"Yeah, I know. But, when I got home tonight, I felt so low I could crawl under the door without opening it. I saw you over here and I just had to talk to you. I know in the past I always felt so much better after I talked to you when I was depressed. Right then, I didn't care what I had promised."

Spike lightly grasped her wrist. "Karen, all I can say is, you'd better think things through clearly. I don't want to see our friendship ended. You've got to get hold of yourself and put things back into perspective. Don't let this guy ruin your life. He just isn't worth it."

Karen lowered her eyes and glanced at her watch. "I . . . I've got to go. Why don't you come over to the house soon? We haven't seen you in a while. Dody is really getting lonesome for you."

He grinned. "I will and thanks. Are you sure it's all right?"

"No one is going to keep Dody's friends away as far as I am concerned."

His face showed no disappointment or anger. "I'll bring her that cycle model that I put together for her."

"Good. We'll see you soon then." With a warm smile, Karen turned and raced across the lawn toward home.

"I'll check the Pumpkin's brakes for you after I'm through with my cycle!" Spike yelled as he watched Karen disappear out of sight.

Chapter 12

Karen sat on a stone park bench and watched Dody race from one piece of playground equipment to another. She was captivated and sometimes confused by the many choices. Sometimes, she would just stand looking around finding it almost beyond her limited capacity to decide which plaything to choose. Karen smiled to herself as she watched her run to the swings. With determination, she pulled her small, squat body up onto the rubber slat and proceeded to pump high into the air. Her short, rust-colored braids blew back from her head. Her face was alight with joy. Dody waved to Karen, a huge grin on her face. Karen waved back and blew her a kiss.

Karen thought how content and happy she looked swinging back and forth high off of the ground having not a care in the world. The same, ever-present pangs of guilt jabbed at her as she watched her sister. The little girl loved life and all of the people that life presented. There was no self-pity, malice, envy, or regret in her makeup. She relished and enjoyed each and every day. Yet, she had so many obstacles to put up with: ill health, retardation, and peoples' prejudices. Dody saw the world through rose-colored glasses and the people in it as perfect. She lived each day with a love and a contentment. Subconsciously, Karen shook her head feeling ashamed of worrying over her small, insignificant troubles.

"Karen, come push me! Come push me!" Dody pleaded as she raced toward the merry-go-round.

"Be right there!" Karen yelled back. For the moment she pushed her cares aside and bounded toward her sister.

A grunt escaped Karen's gritted teeth as she gave the huge metallic monster a shove. Dody squealed with glee, her hands wrapped tightly about the railing.

"Faster, Karen, faster!" she screamed trying to control her giggles.

Catching hold of a metal bar, Karen raced beside the merry-go-round until it turned at a dizzying rate. Her breath expelled in small bursts as she stood heaving, watching Dody spin past. Around and around she went. Karen giggled to herself as she watched her funny little face creased in a huge, joyous grin each time she spun by.

The uneasiness and insecurity that Karen had felt started to lift from her. She was enjoying this outing perhaps even more than Dody herself. The doubts and fears were ignored in the background of her thoughts for the moment and it was just Dody and she blocking out the rest of the world.

Dody pointed her finger. "Karen, stop it and let her on!"

Karen looked around at a shy, beautiful little girl standing beside her watching Dody with envy. The morning sun bounced off of her soft, blonde curls. She looked up with huge, liquid brown eyes the color of chestnuts and smiled. She was a child who could enchant anyone, Karen thought.

Karen leaned down. "Would you like to ride the merry-go-round too?"

The little girl stared shyly down at the ground before her and nodded.

"All right! I think that can be arranged. Do you think we can take on another passenger, Dody?" Karen yelled as she passed by.

"Let her on, Karen! Let her on!" Dody cried.

Snatching the metal rail, Karen braced herself in the hard-packed earth and brought the spinning contraption to a stop. Carefully, she lifted the little girl on to a seat and started it once again. Dody smiled and waved to her new companion. The little girl continued to remain somber, gripping the railing.

Karen stood back, her arms folded, smiling to herself as she watched the two girls catapult around and around. One of them was much younger than the other in age but mentally they were comparable. The little girl's flaxen hair blew in the wind. A jolt of remorse hit at Karen as she realized that this little girl would undoubtedly grow up healthy and normal. No doubt, one day, she would fall in love, marry and have beautiful children of her own. She had a wonderful, fulfilling lifetime ahead of her. On the other hand, Dody would always be frail and mentally handicapped. In later years, she may even have to live in an institution.

Karen bandied her head about in an effort to dispell those thoughts. She could never bear to see Dody sent to an institution.

"Hey, babe!"

Karen's head quickly turned at the sound of the resonant, masculine voice. An excited chill charged through her as she watched Marc lope toward her in the distance. Raising her hand, she waved enthusiastically and then stood back watching him approach. A shock of raven-winged hair fell boyishly over his forehead. He moved in smooth, liquid motions his broad shoulders thrown back. Even from a distance, she marveled at the glistening snow-white teeth of his smile. His long, muscular legs moved him along quickly and he soon stood at her side hardly out of breath. Without a warning, he picked her up and spun her around. Karen screamed with delight as she felt his strong arms encircle her. Finally, he put her down and deposited a small peck on the tip of her nose. Karen drew back giggling breathlessly.

"What was all of that for?" she asked, feeling a rush of blood into her face.

"I just couldn't help it." He put up his hands in a mystical pantomime. "I saw this beautiful vision in the distance. The sun was reflecting off of her auburn hair. Her face looked like an angel's." His hands then made a suggestive undulating motion. "And that figure! Wow! That figure!"

Karen quickly glanced at the two little girls on the merry-go-round with embarrassment. At once, she realized, that they were only aware of the fun that they were having.

"I saw the Pumpkin parked at the curb so I knew you were here."

"I take my little sister to the park at least once a week. She always has a great time."

Marc looked over at the merry-go-round starting to slow down. With an effortless push he sent it spinning again to the delighted shrieks of the two occupants. Brushing his hands together, he walked back to Karen. "I just wanted to stop and ask you a question. It's about the dance. I really would like to take you."

Karen looked up into his appealing deep-blue eyes and melted. Today, he seemed so different to her. The surly arrogance was absent and the sincere charm that he had the day they first met at the Pit was present. Karen had never seen him look so handsome. She knew that there was no way she could possibly refuse him.

"I would really like that," she replied simply, remembering all the years she and her friends went together and all the fun they had.

Reaching out, he took her hand. "You know, babe, you're tops! You're going to be the biggest knockout there. There's not a guy around who's got a girl who can hold a candle to you."

Karen kicked at the dirt self-consciously. "I don't

think it's true, but it's great to hear you say it, anyway."

"Hey, babe, we're going to have a great time. It's the dance of the year. You look your prettiest and I'll pick you up about eight."

"Sounds great!"

"I've got to go. I'm already a half hour late for the Saturday practice. But, when I saw your car here, I just had to stop and ask you. The coach will understand." Placing his thumbs beneath imaginary suspenders, he pushed out his chest. "Wouldn't dare do anything to his star, anyway, would he?"

"Suppose not," Karen replied looking away.

"Hey, those two kids' vehicle is about out of gas. I'd better give them one last quick shove before I leave." Again, he sent the merry-go-round reeling.

"Good looks run in your family, Karen. Your kid sister is as much of a charmer as her older sister. She's going to set the guys back on their heels when she's older." He chuckled looking toward the pretty, little blond-haired girl gripping the rail.

Karen shook her head. "No, Marc, that's not my little sister. The other little girl is my sister, Dody."

He started to laugh but grew sober when he realized that she was serious. "You mean, that girl? . . ." he said self-consciously pointing at Dody. "I mean, I didn't know." Finally, he lowered his head and kicked at the dirt in exasperation.

Karen recognized the look, the prejudice. He was as narrow-minded about Dody as he was about

Spike. A sick feeling waved through her. She made an effort to smile. "Yes, Marc, that's my sister, Dody. Would you like me to stop the merry-go-round and let you meet her?

At that same moment Dody looked up, smiled and waved to him.

Marc ignored her and glanced at his watch. "Hey, I've got to go! The old coach turns purple when anyone is late. Even if I am one of the stars, I'd hate to see him have a stroke."

"I see," Karen said quietly.

He gave her a quick hug and turned abruptly. "I've got to go. See you Friday night at eight if not before." Turning on his heels, he ran to his car waving back at her.

Karen watched him pull away in the maroon Camaro with a shrill screech and speed down the street out of sight. She turned and watched the merry-go-round slowly spin to a stop. Walking over to Dody, she enfolded her in a strong embrace.

Dody grunted at its strength and looked up with a perplexed expression. "Why did you do that, Karen?"

"Just because I wanted to, Dody," she choked. "Just because I wanted to."

Chapter 13

Karen stood in front of the full-length mirror casting a critical eye at the girl looking back at her. Perhaps, her hair would look better if the bangs were pulled over to one side and clipped with a small, gold barrette. Or maybe, an upsweep would be proper; it would make her appear older, more sophisticated. Marc would like that. With a wrinkle of her nose, she removed her hand and allowed her hair to fall back into place. No, it looked too pretentious. It looked just like she didn't want it to look: like a young girl trying very hard to look like an older woman. It looked phoney, somehow.

With a self-agreeing nod, Karen decided to wear it just as she had always worn it the last five years of her life, a straight bang with the back cascading casually down to her shoulders. She swooped the brush through the smooth, lustrous hair and smiled at herself and at the girl in the mirror. After two hours and ten different hair styles, she had at last returned to the usual, everyday one. The one that looked the most like Karen Cooper.

Smoothing the simple, white percale bodice of her dress, Karen smiled with self-satisfaction. She did look dazzling tonight. Her eyes sparkled like diamonds and there was a faint blush in her cheeks denoting excitement and expectation. She wanted Marc to be as proud being seen with her tonight as she would be being seen with him.

Wincing, she recalled his reaction in the park a few days ago when he realized that Dody was her sister. An acrid taste filtered into her mouth and she frowned, turning away from the eyes in the reflection. She was proud that Dody was her sister; she would never deny her.

Karen looked back at the image an expression of bewilderment on her face. Was Marc as narrow about accepting handicapped people as he was about believing that a boy and girl could not have a platonic relationship? Was any relationship worth all of the sacrifices, all of the compromises, that she was going through recently?

Shaking her head emphatically, Karen stepped back from the mirror noticing a tear straining to erupt from the corner of her eye. Awkwardly, she muffed at her eyes and nose trying to spare what little makeup she had applied for this evening. Tonight, when he came to pick her up, he would meet Dody personally. No one, no matter how cold, could resist the charm of the little girl.

Karen dried her eyes with the palm of her hand and stepped out into the hall. Carefully, gripping the bannister for support, she descended the steps into the awaiting accolades of her admiring family.

"Oh, Karen, you look lovely," Mrs. Cooper sighed, embracing her warmly.

"She'll be the prettiest one at the dance, no doubt about it," Mr. Cooper boasted pulling his pipe from his clenched teeth, depositing a fatherly kiss on her cheek.

Karen looked down as she felt a tug on her gown. Dody looked up holding her doll Katrina. Katrina, with her one black-button eye, raveled-yellow yarn hair, and torn foot reminded Karen of Dody. They seemed to be meant for each other. Both of them were handicapped and somewhat bedraggled yet both of them offered an unselfish, no-strings-attached love.

"Dody, be careful, so you don't muss Karen's dress," Mrs. Cooper warned.

Dody looked up her eyes blinking in awe. "Karen, you look just like the angel we put on top of our Christmas tree!"

Struggling to swallow, Karen leaned down and swooped the little girl into her arms, crushing her to her not caring what damage she did to her dress or to her appearance. For several moments, she held her close without saying a word.

Finally, Mrs. Cooper walked around and looked up startled as she noticed the tears streaming from her daughter's eyes. "Hon, what is it? Are you all right?"

Releasing the little girl, Karen straightened self-consciously and managed a pained smile. "Yes . . . yes, I'm all right. I . . . I guess it's just the excitement of tonight and . . . and everything, that's all."

147

Mr. Cooper cleared his throat endeavoring to ease the atmosphere. "And tonight," he said with firmness, "we all get to meet this great young man you've been telling us about for weeks. I hope he measures up to all of our expectations."

"Oh, he will, dad! Marc is a wonderful person!" Karen looked away from his concerned, doubting eyes. "He's been wanting to meet you all for such a long time, but with school and track practice and everything, he's just been too busy."

"Well," Mr. Cooper replied with a revealing frown, "I don't know if . . ."

"Let's all go into the living room and wait for him," Mrs. Cooper interjected quickly with a warning glance to her husband. "I'm sure he'll be here any minute now. It's almost eight o'clock."

"Sounds good." Karen encircled Dody's shoulders and they all walked together into the next room to wait for the new boy in town.

Karen thumbed through the pages of a magazine pretending to be absorbed in it with interest. She squirmed uncomfortably in her chair well aware that her mother was looking worried, the mechanical movements of her fingers flying as she knitted. Her father stared at her with concern over the sports page of the newspaper. Only Dody had given up the vigil as the clock struck nine and had fallen asleep on the floor cradling Katrina in her arms.

Karen bit into the flesh of the inside of her cheek as she heard the chimes denote the late hour. A wet film coated her eyes as she looked at the colored pages presenting themselves in smeared distortions. Silently, she reprimanded herself for the tears. Painfully, she realized that she had done more crying in the brief period since she had met Marc than in the preceding year. It didn't seem to be a healthy omen for a relationship, she was sure of that. No matter what had happened, he could have called. There was never a reason not to phone. She thought back to his casual thoughtlessness about calling over two months ago.

Karen started as her father's voice broke the silence.

"If you wouldn't mind an old duffer, I'd be honored to escort such a pretty young lady to the dance. It would take me but a minute to drag my old tux out of moth balls." Looking over to her, he tried his best to smile.

Karen looked up seeing his blurred image and returned the smile. "It's great of you to offer, dad, and I love you for it. Maybe next time, okay?"

"Any time, sweetheart," he replied trying to camouflage the hurt he was feeling for her at the moment.

"Maybe . . . maybe he had car trouble. He might still come," Mrs. Cooper offered hopefully.

"Do you honestly think so, mom?" Karen questioned.

Mrs. Cooper lowered her eyes and forlornly shook her head.

"Well," Karen said as she bounced to her feet, "I'm not going to sit here and moan about it all evening. I'm going to get into the Pumpkin and putt putt right over the the Central High gymnasium. Spike and Sandy will be there." She tried her best to sound ebullient.

"Good idea!" Mr. Cooper said tossing his paper aside. "If your friend comes after you leave we'll say you went on without him!" He emphasized the last part feeling that some retaliation must be taken against this young culprit for causing his daughter such heartache.

Quickly, before her fragile emotions crumbled, Karen grabbed a sweater, kissed her parents goodnight, and walked out into the balmy night air. The delicate-sweet scent of spring filled her nostrils and she breathed deep. The zealous inhalation was as much for the relief of escaping from the pitying stares of her parents as it was for the pleasant aroma of the night.

Karen dug beneath the floor mat for her keys. With a turn of the wrist, she welcomed the easy, unassuming purr of the Pumpkin. It sounded relaxed and familiar compared to the threatening, powerful roar of Marc's Camaro. With a sigh, she turned her head to back out of the drive when squinting through the darkness, Karen saw the tall, lumbersome silhouette of her good friend, Spike as he left his house. Glancing quickly down at her gown she looked up and watched his easy approach.

He leaned into the window and she smelled his clean, just-scrubbed scent. "I've never seen you look prettier," Spike said smiling.

Karen executed a small, in-place curtsy. "Why, thank you kind sir. That's very gallant of you."

"It's really a great night tonight, huh? I've never smelled the air so sweet." He looked skyward. "That moon looks like a huge, luminous disc caught on a swath of blue velvet."

"Why, that's beautiful, Spike. I didn't know you could speak like that."

"Ah, shucks, ma'm, twern't nothin'; musta' read it somewhar' or somethin'."

Karen giggled. "Will you get serious?" She lightly reprimanded him even though she was actually relishing the easy feeling of being with him.

He straightened and attempted to look sober. "All right, I'm serious."

She looked up through the darkness and smiled at him. "You look real fine yourself, Spike."

He pulled at the lapels of his tuxedo. "I do have clothes other than T-shirts and jeans, you know. Once in a while I'll spruce up."

"I take it that you're on your way to the dance, then."

He nodded. "Yeah, I thought I'd go over for a while." He scratched beneath the red bush of coarse, red hair. "I'd feel kind of out of place riding my cycle over there with a suit and tie on, however."

"Why . . ." Karen hesitated momentarily in deliberation. ". . . Why don't you hop in and go with me?"

"What about Marc? Aren't you going with him?"

Karen looked shyly away. "I was. I mean, I waited for over an hour. I . . . I guess he's just not going to show up." She sighed and forced herself to smile. "So, I just decided to jump into the Pumpkin and go on over. I'd be glad to give you a lift if you want it."

"Are you sure it's okay?" He shuffled his feet nervously in the dirt. "I mean after what you told me about what the jock made you promise . . ."

Karen frowned. "At the moment I'm not at all that concerned about it. He didn't seem to care enough to pick me up on time or to phone and tell me the reason he was going to be late."

"So, I guess you're telling me that it's okay if I hop in and ride over with you."

Karen hesitated for a moment as she bit into her lower lip. "Yes, that's what I'm telling you. I really wish you would ride over with me, Spike, to keep me company." Her voice was almost beseeching. "Frankly, I'm feeling pretty down tonight."

Abruptly, Spike executed a low, sweeping bow. "At your service m' lady. It would be my pleasure."

Karen giggled and leaned over to open the door on the passenger side of the car. "Great! Let's go!"

Karen waited for him to get settled and then she eased the Pumpkin out of the drive and onto the street.

They both rode for several minutes without speaking. The contented drone of the Pumpkin provided a suitable background for their separate thoughts.

Finally, Spike cleared his throat uneasily. "Hey, this is kind of off the subject, Karen, but where's Sandy been hanging out lately? You and she used to be as inseparable as the Bobbsey Twins."

Karen sighed, looking up into the darkness trying to distinguish the features of his face as she drove. "I know. I really miss her, too. It just seems that lately she goes her way and I go mine. I guess we really don't have that much in common any more."

"Not that much in common! Did my ears hear that correctly?" Spike cried incredulously. "The two gals that couldn't or wouldn't make a move for years without getting reassurance or permission from the other via the phone! The two gals that led Central High's cheering section for the last two years! The two gals who were always together so much it was feared that they would eventually fuse into Siamese twins!"

"Okay, okay," Karen cried holding up her hands in surrender. "I get your point. We still do have a lot in common. It . . . it just seems that ever since I started dating Marc, we sort of . . . well, sort of drifted into separate paths. Do you know what I mean?"

"Yeah." His voice was low, barely audible. "Yeah, I know what you mean. The jock keeps you pretty busy, I guess."

A strange twinge of resentment prodded her. She was confused as to why his last statement bothered her. Shaking off the feeling, she composed herself. "No, I just mean Marc and I have so much fun together, do so many exciting things that . . ." She shrugged. ". . . well, it just seems we don't have time for other people."

"Yeah, I've noticed that."

Karen swung her head around abruptly and stared up into his shaded face trying to decide what the subtle nuances were underlying his last statement.

"He's still been doing pretty well in the meets, I hear. He's not burning up the track like he did earlier in the season against Havenville, but he's still placing.

Karen nodded trying her best to appear proud. An uneasy feeling overcame her as she recalled his late hours, breaking training, and the many times he missed practice. It was evident that some of the skill that he had at the first part of the season was absent now. "He'll find his stride again. Might even improve his record."

"That would be great." His voice was empty of enthusiasm.

A tension-filled pause prevailed between them for a moment but subsided as they reached the gymnasium.

The music of the latest popular hits beat at their brains as they entered the gymnasium. The dance floor was inundated with writhing, gyrating bodies. On a riser, in the midst of the gaiety, was a DJ with a profusion of elaborate stereo and sound equipment. The music seemed to reach, invade, and saturate every niche in the huge, old edifice. A distraught look covered the faces of some of the faculty members as they could feel their ears being physically assaulted. However, Dr. Melford was not among them. He was clearly enjoying his very own rendition of a disco number with his wife among the mingling, jostling students. Spike and Karen paused for a moment to watch, marveling at his agility and skill on the dance floor. Finally, they looked up to each other and nodded their approval. Karen, quickly recalled her meeting in Dr. Melford's office and the concern and compassion he had shown that day. He was, she assured herself, a very nice understanding man. He was very much like her own grandfather. Although, at the moment, he looked anything but a grandfather. She giggled to herself; it remained undetected beneath the overwhelming sound.

Spike guided her easily to a table. Through the oppressive sound he skillfully charaded his intentions. He was going after punch and would return shortly.

Karen nodded and seated herself. At once, she caught familiar faces through the dizzying strobe lights. Her old friends greeted her with enthusiasm. She waved back enjoying seeing them again. The evening had started out to be such a tragedy, but thanks to Spike she was actually enjoying herself now.

Through the screen of crepe paper bunting, bobbing heads, and stereo equipment, she caught the figure of Sandy sitting alone across the gym executing her ever present habit of jabbing at her glasses. A moment of longing cut into her seeing the familiar face. She missed her old friend even more than she had realized. It was as though she had been away on a long, strange trip ever since Marc had come to town.

For a moment she felt that, at last, she had returned and her life would, once again, be put into the right perspective. It was as though she had found some missing pieces to a jigsaw puzzle that made up her life.

Just as Spike arrived with the punch, the overzealous DJ called a time out and all the bustling, energetic dancers left the floor.

"All right! Here you go! You could have your choice of grape, strawberry, raspberry, boysenberry, blackberry, gooseberry, and Chuck Berry punch. I took advantage of my position as your escort tonight and chose strawberry for you."

Karen laughed. "You dope! You're kidding, of course."

He nodded. "Yeah, afraid so. Actually, there's just this diluted swill of lime and ginger ale topped with little floating icebergs."

Karen giggled feeling quite relaxed. From across the gym her eye caught Sandy once again. She winced as she noticed how lonely she appeared. Abruptly, she stood and waved to her. Sandy craned her neck and squinted into the confusion of lights and jostling bodies. Karen smiled as she saw her respond with an enthusiastic wave of her hand and awkwardly clamber down the bleachers on vascillating high heels. "She saw me," Karen exclaimed excitedly. "She's coming over!"

"Great! It'll be like old times again."

Karen's smile faded as she nodded. "Yes, it'll be like old times again." They both laughed as they watched Sandy manage her way through the sea of bodies toward them.

When she finally arrived her corsage had only a few limp petals left and her glasses were slid to the tip of her nose. "For crying out loud!" she panted, "That's like going through the Battle of Bunker Hill!"

Spike patted her on the back and Karen pulled her close in a warm embrace.

"There for a while I didn't know if we'd ever see you again. You were just swallowed up."

"I know," she said pushing her glasses back up onto her nose and then taking a stance of a boxer her fists doubled. "It was either them or me."

Both Karen and Spike laughed at the disheveled girl good-naturedly.

Sandy looked down at her corsage and plucked off the few remaining petals and handed them to them. "Here, have a souvenir of tonight's bout."

Spike brought a chair and gallantly lowered Sandy into it. "Here, you sit down and I'll go get you some of that swamp water to quench your thirst."

Sandy looked up at him and sighed. "Thank you, kind sir. I would be very grateful."

Spike laughed, shook his head, and headed toward the punch table.

Sandy sat there for a moment self-consciously smoothing out the wrinkles in her organdy dress.

Karen reached out and took her hand.

"Sandy, I want to apologize for being such a fool lately."

Sandy opened her mouth prepared to speak but Karen shook her head. "No . . . no! Let me finish. It may be the one and only apology you'll ever get from me." Her expression grew solemn. "I've treated you very badly the last couple of weeks. I've been rude and thoughtless . . . and I'm sorry."

Sandy poked at Karen playfully. "Oh, forget it, Karen. I understand. You were going through a lot right then. All I wanted to do is let you know that I was there whenever you needed me."

"Just like always."

"Yeah," she smiled, "just like always."

Karen hit her forehead with the palm of her hand. "I'm such a dope! I have taken you and Spike for granted for so long. I just knew that no matter what may happen you would always be there. I don't know why you guys even put up with me."

Sandy nudged her with an elbow and repositioned her glasses. "Because, you dope, that's what real friends are for. We both know, that in a crisis, you would do the same thing for us. It's always been that way."

"I know." She smiled thoughtfully. "Anyway, I just want to say thanks for this time and all of the others in the past."

Sandy waved her hand to dismiss the seriousness. "Let's cut out all of this sentimental tripe. What I want to know is, has it finally happened?"

"Has what finally happened?"

"Is there something going on between you and Spike?"

Karen reared back and looked at her friend incredulously. "I can't believe you! You are still trying to play matchmaker."

Sandy shrugged. "Well, what was I to think?" She made a wide sweep with her hands. "Here you are, you and Spike, together at the biggest bash of the year." She looked around. "And I don't see a thing of tall, dark, and arrogant."

Karen shook her head. "Spike was just nice enough to be my escort tonight, that's all. It was either him or my dad."

A disappointed expression settled over Sandy's face. "So, it's still on between you and Marc? Right?"

"I . . . I really don't know. He didn't show up tonight."

"Didn't show up!" Sandy screamed disbelievingly. "What do you mean?"

"Just that. He never came to pick me up. I waited and then I decided to just come on without him."

"That nerd!" Sandy placed her hands on her hips with a huff of exasperation. "Do you mean he didn't even call?"

Karen shook her head.

"Well, in some ways I'm glad. Now, at least, you know his true colors. I had him pretty well pegged in the hall at school the other day."

Karen bit into her lower lip so hard she winced.

"I don't know, Sandy. Sometimes, he can be so kind and so gentle. He can also be very exciting to be with." She shrugged. "And then he can change and be just as surly and conceited. I just never know how he's going to be from one time to the next."

"Who needs that aggravation?" Sandy shrugged. "Life is complicated enough without that."

"I know, but I still have a feeling for him. I just can't help it. When I'm near him I get all warm and tingly."

"You can have the same effect with measles," Sandy stated doggedly.

Karen threw her head back and giggled. "Oh, you're impossible."

"All right, m' lady, here's your refreshment." Spike executed a deep bow and presented Sandy a paper cup of punch.

Sandy rolled her eyes back into her head and moaned, a euphoric expression on her face. "I swear, I've died and gone to heaven."

Karen and Spike laughed at her inanity.

"Well, well, the happy trio."

Karen, Spike, and Sandy swung around to Marc Rodgers glowering down upon them.

"You didn't waste any time jumping right in, did you Cycle Jockey?" His eyes narrowed menacingly as he stared at Spike.

"Do you want to interpret that, Superstar?" Spike countered.

"To put it in simple language that all three of you can understand: 'cut in,' 'knifed in the back,' 'took advantage of.' Do you understand now?"

Spike stood there his hands clenched in tight, hard knots. "Just hold on there . . ." A flush invaded his face.

Karen jumped to her feet and positioned herself in the middle of the two adversaries. "Now wait just a minute. I don't want any scene here, tonight." She raised her hands and swung her head from one to the other. "Now, both of you just cool off a minute and we'll get all of this straightened out."

Sandy sat there sipping her punch her eyes bulging beneath the thick lens.

"There's nothing to straighten out. I'm a little late picking up my date and this character butts in and takes advantage of the situation. It's very easy to understand."

Spike lurched forward and hesitated battling to control his temper.

"That isn't how it happened at all," Karen assured him. "I waited for you and when I finally assumed that you had no intention of coming I decided to go on by myself. It just so happened that I met Spike outside as I was ready to pull out of the drive in the Pumpkin and we decided to go together."

"Yeah, I'll just bet!" Marc's mouth was twisted into a snarl.

"Just tell me, what did you expect her to do? Wait around until midnight for you?" Spike queried angrily.

"Yeah, as a matter of fact, that's exactly what I

expect her to do," Marc retaliated.

Spike nodded in Marc's direction. "I can't believe this guy! He must be reincarnated from the Victorian age."

Karen, embarrassingly, looked around pleased that the music was camouflaging much of the loud, vocal argument. "I'm sorry, Marc, but I'm not going to wait around for you or anyone who doesn't have the decency to phone and explain why he's late."

"I just got home a little while ago. I was taking some curves over at Pineview with some of the guys. I wasn't satisfied with the acceleration so I tore into my carburetor to make an adjustment."

"That means you missed track practice again, right?"

Marc shrugged uncaringly.

"And just what was I supposed to do in the meantime?"

"I lost track of time, that's all. Why don't you sue me?" He threw his hands up in a gesture of futility.

Karen glanced back to Spike and Sandy with uncertainty. "Maybe, we should discuss this at another time."

"There just may not be another time."

Karen looked up abruptly noting the cold warning in his piercing, blue eyes. It was all she could do to control her panic as she surveyed his handsome face. He stood there tall and rigid his pitch-black hair touseled wildly over his forehead. His swarthy complexion contrasted becomingly with the light blue of his tuxedo. Karen swallowed with difficulty and replied. "What . . . what do you mean by that?"

"It doesn't take any genius to figure that out, babe," he sneered. He jabbed a thumb into the ruffles of his shirt front. "I don't need this. Your old man gave me a hassle about being late when I went to pick you up. You went on without me with your 'old buddy,' the Cycle Jockey. I'd say you've pretty well made your choice."

Spike, automatically tensed as he absorbed the sarcasm coming from Marc.

"As far as I'm concerned, it's over." He turned abruptly and glanced back over his shoulder. "I hope you have fun riding on the back of a motorcycle."

Karen felt her throat constrict as she watched the handsome boy stalk away from her and immediately flash a smile at the first girl he saw. "Well," she said feebly, "I guess that's that."

"And good riddance, I'd say," Sandy chimed in looking over at Marc already engaged in an animated conversation with a pretty girl.

Spike pressed Karen's arm. "You okay?"

She nodded but looked away. "Yeah, I'm okay. I guess it's for the best. I'm sorry he just can't understand that we're friends."

"How's about shakin' it up on the dance floor, then?"

Karen shrugged. "Thanks, Spike, but not right now. Why don't you and Sandy go ahead? I think I'll sit this one out."

Spike turned to Sandy. "How's about it?"

"With pleasure!" She jumped up and handed Karen her empty paper cup.

Karen forced herself to smile as she watched the two of them maneuver their way out onto the crowded dance floor. Out of the corner of her eye she watched Marc charm one girl after another. She told herself she didn't care. She told herself he was narrow-minded and egotistical and she was glad to be rid of him. But, she could not help that sick, empty feeling churning at the pit of her stomach. This surely was a night she wouldn't forget.

Chapter 14

Karen sat deep in the soft velour cushion of the living room divan chewing on the eraser of her pencil trying to decipher a passage from the "Canterbury Tales." Dody was sitting at her feet with Katrina cradled in her arms. She was absorbed in rocking the disheveled rag doll, its one black-button eye still hanging delicately by a thread.

For the first time in months Karen found that she was able to concentrate. The invisible shield in her brain had finally evaporated and school and life in general came back into focus. She found it amazingly easy to understand her class work and to accomplish her homework quickly and accurately without the distraction and constant strain that the new boy in town had imposed upon her. Just in the last week she had aced three out of her five tests. Even the sometimes unintelligible Spanish phrases started to make some sense to her and she now offered ready answers much to the delight of her instructor, Señor Gonzales.

She was pleased with her academic reawakening

for it had come none too soon. The middle of May was upon her and school would be over the first week of June. She would be a senior then and would have to do some serious thinking about her future.

Relationships with her friends and family had vastly improved and were almost normal. Without the hectic and demanding schedule of cheerleading and following the team she was able to catch up on much of her work that she had neglected in the past. Karen's parents were pleased that their daughter had broken off with Marc Rodgers. It was their consensus, even though they said nothing to her, that he was not a good influence on her. Since the very first day she had seen him in the school cafeteria she had seemed to cease to function as the responsible, happy girl that they had always known. Mr. Cooper would puff upon his pipe and look contentedly over to her, pleased that his daughter was "back" with them again. Mrs. Cooper and Karen joked and laughed together and were closer than ever. Life was back to normal.

Karen looked up as the chimes of the doorbell sounded. She checked her watch and scooted her stocking feet out from under her. Tucking her English Literature text in the crook of her arm, she hurried to the door. A ready smile coated her face for Sandy had called an hour ago to announce that she was on her way over. She swung the door open and her smile faded and she looked up into Marc Rodgers blue, disarming eyes.

"Hi, babe," he said greeting her casually.

Karen stood there for a moment too surprised to respond.

His hands were buried in the side pockets of his beige jacket. "Could I talk to you?"

She continued to stare up at him. "Why? What about?"

He lifted his shoulders. "I can't get into it out here. Do you mind if I come in?"

"I haven't even seen you for two weeks. There's really nothing left to say, Marc. You said it all the night of the dance." She was surprised how calm her voice sounded even though her heart was racing. She tried to smile. "Let's just part company without any more words . . . any more explanations. Okay?" She started to close the door.

He blocked it with a shoulder. "Just give me five minutes. That's all I ask for . . . just five minutes."

Karen closed her eyes and sighed deeply. "All right." She moved aside so he could enter.

As they entered the living room Mr. Cooper looked up from his paper and frowned. Mrs. Cooper came in from the kitchen wiping her hands on her apron.

Karen stood there with Marc, feeling quite ill at ease. "Mom . . . dad, I would like you to meet Marc Rodgers."

Mr. Cooper remained seated and nodded toward the boy, his pipe clenched between his teeth. "We've met, Karen." He cleared his throat uneasily. "That night of the dance two weeks ago."

Marc's face failed to display any emotion. He, in

turn, nodded to Mr. Cooper.

Mrs. Cooper stepped forward and presented her hand. "Very nice to meet you, Marc."

"Thank you." he replied.

"And, Marc," Karen continued, "this is my sister, Dody." She encircled Dody's shoulders and brought her to stand next to her. "You saw her with me a while back in the park. Do you remember?"

Marc's eyes surveyed the little retarded girl from top to toe. She grimaced and he flinched stepping back nervously. "Yeah . . . I remember."

Dody walked to him and looked up. She smiled and presented Katrina to him. "This is my doll, Katrina. Do you want to hold her?"

Marc stared at the little girl suspiciously and finally shook his head.

"You're tall," she said. "You're really tall."

He nodded and looked warily over to Karen.

"I love you, Marc!" Dody screamed encircling his long legs.

For a moment it appeared as if the boy would try to escape from his skin. A pained, desperate expression emerged upon his face. He recoiled as he looked down on the top of the little girl's head embracing his legs.

Karen walked over and easily pulled Dody away. She kneeled looking up at her sister. "Marc likes you, too, Dody. Don't you, Marc?"

His head nodded mechanically as his face blanched.

"See," Karen assured her, "I told you so."

Dody smiled and cuddled Katrina close to her.

"Could we . . . could we talk in private, Karen?" Marc asked.

Karen nodded. "Sure. We can go into my room." She looked over to the worried faces of her parents. "We'll only be a few minutes. Marc just has something to talk to me about."

Hesitantly, Mr. Cooper nodded his approval watching them closely until they were hidden behind Karen's closed door.

Nervously, Marc rubbed his hands together.

"Would you like to sit down?" Karen asked offering him the stool to her vanity.

He shrugged. "No . . . no, thanks. I'll stand."

"All right. Now, what is it?"

"I . . . I got canned today. Coach Gordon told me to pack my things in my locker and get out." The smug, cynical expression was absent from his face this time.

Karen looked up seeing the searing hurt in his eyes. "I'm so sorry, Marc."

Carelessly, he raised his hands and let them drop to his sides. "Oh, who needs it! I'm tired of running my guts out for nothing anyway."

Karen sat on the edge of her bed not knowing what to say. She wanted to help him but right now she felt an overpowering need to escape from him.

"Aren't you even going to ask why I was kicked off the squad?"

She answered without looking at him. "I don't have to. You got kicked off for missing too many practices and breaking training."

"Yeah, that about sums it up," he said dejectedly.

"I'm sorry, Marc, but what did you expect? You've broken training several times as well as missed practices. You couldn't expect him just to keep you just because of a record you set at the beginning of the season."

He lowered his head and sat down beside her. "I suppose not. I suppose it was just a matter of time before the axe fell."

Karen looked up feeling sorrow for him. She laid her hand against his cheek. "I feel sorry it happened. You were very good at the start of the season."

He looked into her eyes and leaned forward to kiss her. In one motion she parried away from him and stood. "It's too late for that, Marc."

"Too late!" he cried incredulously. "What do you mean, too late?"

"Have you developed amnesia or something? What about two weeks ago? What about all of the horrible things you said to me? What about the ridicule you've put me through? What about your stupid jealousy?" Abruptly, she turned and headed for the door. "I don't need all of that. My life is just now starting to straighten out again. There's no use talking about all of this. It's just better that we call it quits right now before the hurt gets any worse."

"Karen, let's give it another chance. I need our relationship now more than ever. I need you to help me through this time. You've got to help me!" His voice broke and he ashamedly turned his back.

Slowly, Karen turned and watched him as he stood, head bowed, looking defeated, alone. "I just can't, Marc. I can't go back and forth like this. It tears me apart."

"Please, Karen. I'll change. Getting kicked off the track squad was like a hard punch in the gut. It woke me up to a lot of things." Swinging around to her, she detected a glaze on the surface of his flawless, blue eyes. The cocksure arrogance was gone. The cutting, wounding cynicism was gone. He was now just a boy reaching out for someone. Karen's conscience reminded her of the ridicule, the hurt, the risk.

"I . . . I just don't know. My life has been so wrong ever since we met. I want to help you, but I've got to help myself, too. We don't seem to make a good team. We constantly battle each other. We seem to want different things." She looked up to him her face etched with pain. "It just won't work."

"It will work! I realize how important you are to me. I'll prove it to you if you'll give me another chance." Slowly, he walked toward her appearing humble, defeated. Reaching out, he tilted her head back and peered down into her eyes.

Karen fought the old, familiar feeling of yielding, of surrender. She closed her eyes to avoid looking up at him, but when she opened them he was there. "I . . . I just don't know. I want to help you but I don't want to get hurt all over again. I am so tired of crying!"

Marc lowered his head and met her lips.

Karen felt herself being swept up in a strange ecstasy. It was as though her conscience was being pushed aside even as the warnings were echoing in her brain.

Finally, she backed away and looked up to him. She licked her lips nervously knowing that her next question would decide whether their relationship would ever succeed. "And what about Spike?"

A scowl, immediately, came to his face. "What about Spike?"

"Are you ready to accept that two people of the opposite sex can just be good friends? Are you ready to accept Spike's and my friendship? Are you ready to understand that I need to talk and confide in him and he in me?"

He threw his head back and laughed. "You've got to be kidding! We're not going through all of that again. I believe what I've always believed: there's no such thing as a platonic relationship." The lines around his mouth grew taut, unyielding.

"Then nothing has changed," she said simply. She reached out and pressed Marc's arm. "I like you, Marc. I like you very much. In fact, for months, you've been about the only thing I've thought about."

"Well then?"

She sighed and released his arm. "I like you very much but I don't like some of the things you do. I don't like the way you think. I don't like your narrowness. You don't understand any more about Spike and me than you do about Dody." She smiled wistfully. "I sort of feel sorry for you.

You're going to miss out on meeting and knowing a lot of super people by the way you think."

"Get off of your soap box, Karen, and give it to me straight in twenty-five words or less."

She nodded. "Okay, here it is straight. Even though I like you and think you're handsome, fun, and talented, I will not give up my friendship with Spike for our relationship. I want and need others in my life even if you think you don't."

"Do you realize what you're saying? You're giving up something real special for . . . for that Cycle Jockey!"

Karen smiled. "That Cycle Jockey, as you call him, has been one of my best friends for ten years. If you can't understand that I . . . I feel sorry for you."

A ruddy hue crept up his throat and into his face. He stood there his hands clenched into tight balls. "Don't feel sorry for me, babe! I thought we had something special and could keep it going until I leave for college, and maybe even longer." With that, he stomped to the door, swung it open, and walked haughtily through it.

He passed Mr. and Mrs. Cooper and Dody without speaking.

Karen suddenly felt a sense of relief as she detected the less than subtle closing of the front door.

Mr. Cooper looked back over his shoulder quizzically. "Get everything settled, Karen?"

"Yes, dad," Karen said soberly, "We finally got everything settled."

Chapter 15

Karen sat in the large, empty living room thumbing through a teen magazine. Her thoughts ran the gamut from the end of school to what would lay in store for her for the future. She was now a senior and it was more than time to get serious about school. The last year could be the most important of the four. During the last month, she had pulled her grades up to respectability but realized that next year she had to try even harder, it being the last one before college. She regretted that she would not be a part of the cheerleading squad next year. She had always been an exuberant supporter of the school. But, in some ways she thought, perhaps it had been a blessing in disguise. Now, she would have far more time to concentrate on her studies and the really important things related to school.

Karen smiled to herself and sighed realizing that she had just read an entire page in the magazine without understanding one word of it. Tossing it aside, she knew that her concentration was futile today. She shrugged casually. Anyway, what could she expect the day after school was out?

The chimes of the doorbell interrupted her thoughts and she eased her feet off of the couch and proceeded to the door. She opened it and smiled instantly as she saw Sandy.

"How you doin'? Can you believe that we're seniors at last?"

With a gleeful shriek, she embraced her old friend and they stood for a moment relishing each other's closeness. "Come in, Sandy!" Karen cried grasping her hand. "I was hoping you'd drop by. I feel kind of restless suddenly."

Sandy nudged her glasses back up on to her nose and executed a toothy grin. "I know what you mean. A person burns the midnight oil for a couple of weeks cramming for exams and then suddenly, Zap!, it's all over." She made a punctuated gesture into the air. "It takes a little time for a person's brain to come back down to earth. I think it's a little like jet lag."

"I know." Karen hit the side of her head in agreement.

"By the way, Karen, can I bring in an old pal of yours?"

"A what?" Karen asked perplexed. She knew of Sandy's bent to humor and tricks. She prepared herself for anything.

Suddenly, a big sandy-haired, freckled-faced boy emerged from behind a bush next to the house. "Guess who!" he yelled cupping his hands to his mouth. Slowly, he lumbered forward his face lighted with a huge, unpretentious grin.

"This is like old times," Karen cried cheerfully. "Both of you come on in."

The three friends seated themselves in the living room.

"Is Dody here?" Spike asked. "I told you I'd bring over that model for her."

"She's in her bedroom playing with her doll, Katrina. I'll call her out in just a minute. But first, I want Sandy to tell us both the great news in her life." She winked slyly at Spike. "She's going to come clean and confess why neither of us have seen anything of her the last two weeks." Karen's eyes swung toward Sandy.

"Oh, I've got you curious, have I?" She patted her hair ostentatiously. "Well, I've been very busy. Now that I've lost six pounds I've been having to fight the boys off with a stick."

"That's great!" Karen paused not quite sure if she were serious. She noticed the unusual sparkle in her eyes. "You mean you've got someone who . . ."

Sandy nodded with a victorious smile. "I met this great guy in Science Club. He's really neat! It's funny how I've suddenly developed this insatiable interest in dissecting frogs and classifying plants."

Karen giggled and clapped her hands together. "That's sensational!" She reached out and took Sandy's hand. "I'm so happy for you."

"Yeah," she said dreamily, "ain't love grand?" At last she shrugged. "Well, I think maybe when our relationship cooled a bit it gave me time to sort of discover myself." She looked down at the floor thoughtfully. "Maybe I was always trying to live my life through you, Karen. I don't know. At least, now I know that I can do a lot of things on my own."

"I couldn't be more thrilled for you!"

Spike lurched forward and patted Sandy on the back. "Thataway to go, Sandy!"

Sandy swung around and met Spike's eyes. "Yeah, well you had your chance, you know." She poked a finger beneath her chin in a pose.

Spike bit into the side of his lip in a grim expression. Abruptly, he dropped to his knees and grabbed Sandy's hand. "Give me another chance fair damsel. I will do anything for another chance!"

Sandy pulled her hand away and patted her hair demurely. "Sorry, Buster, you had your chance. Anyway, that cycle of yours could never be as exciting as a microscope."

Spike collapsed to the floor in a fit of anguish. "It's over! It's over!" He yelled. "It's over even before it began!"

Karen wiped the tears of laughter from her eyes. She looked down at Spike lying without movement on the floor. "I don't have to ask how you've been. You've been cracking the books the last two weeks." She glanced over to Sandy. "Probably got straight A's again," She said wistfully.

"Yeah," Sandy winced, "Isn't it disgusting?"

Spike sat up and hunched his shoulders. "I can't help it if my folks gave birth to a genius."

Both Karen and Sandy shrieked in exasperation

and started to pummel the boy with throw pillows.

Spike threw his hands over his face to counteract the barrage. At last he groaned and crumpled back to the floor. Both girls continued beating him with the pillows.

At last, he waved his hands feebly in surrender. He got to his feet and his face flushed. "Boy, when you females go after a guy, you really go after him!"

Karen felt buoyant with happiness. She knew that this was exactly where she belonged—right here with her two best friends. They made her feel secure and wanted and she relished their advice and company. She loved to laugh and act ridiculous with them. She felt comfortable and knew that they were not judging her. They accepted her as she accepted them. She knew, at this moment, no matter how separate their paths would be in the future they would always remain friends. She winced inwardly. It was a shame Marc could not understand that. He would miss out on many warm, valuable relationships.

Karen's face grew pensive for a moment as she raised her hand. "I just want to say something to the both of you." She dug nervously at a thumbnail. "I don't want to get sloppy or anything but I just want you both to know how very lucky I feel having you both for friends. We've been close for so long and now that we're going into our final year of high school we're going to need each other's support more than ever." She looked over into Sandy's mist-coated eyes and smiled. "I vow

179

that I will never take our friendship for granted ever again." She swung around to face Spike. "And to you, Spike, I just want to say, 'thanks.' Thanks for always being there whenever I needed you. Thanks for not preaching to me. Thanks for just being you." Reaching out, she clasped his arm.

Sandy snorted and rushed to Karen with her arms open. For several moments the two embraced both of them sniffling on each other's shoulders. Spike looked toward the ceiling in consternation and, patronizingly, patted both of them on the back.

Finally, Karen extricated herself from the embrace and dabbed at the corners of her eyes with a knuckle. "Now," she sniffed, "I'll go get Dody." She turned and left the room.

Dody entered the room clutching her favorite doll, Katrina. Added yarn had unraveled and fallen from Katrina's head and the one good eye was hanging tenuously from a black thread. At the sight of Spike, Dody executed a shrill warhoop and bounded forward landing in his arms.

He received her with open arms. "How you been doin', Punkin?" He nuzzled her head. "Gee, I've missed you!"

A hug ending in an elongated grunt, Dody reared back studying him. "I not seen you for a long time. Where you been?"

Spike looked briefly to Karen and then back again to the little girl. "I don't really have any excuses for neglecting my favorite girl. I promise to visit you real regular from now on. Okay?"

Dody's head bobbed up and down in agreement. "Visit all the time, Spike. Okay?"

Spike grinned and punched her playfully in the stomach. "You can bet on it, Punkin!"

Dody grew thoughtful for a moment. "I got a s'prise for you while you gone."

"Surprise, for me?" Spike laid his palm on his chest. "What is it? I really dig surprises!"

With deliberate pride, Dody took a sheet of paper and a pencil and knelt on the carpet next to the coffee table. Enthusiastically, she grimaced and nodded toward the paper. Laboriously, with care and with her tongue poked out of the corner of her mouth in concentration, she printed her name: D— O—D—Y. After she finished, she handed the paper to him and gave him one last hug.

Spike looked at the hesitant and carefully written name and smiled warmly. "Hey, that's really fine. Thanks a lot! I'm going to tape that on my bedroom mirror so I can see it all of the time." He pulled her to him and kissed her on the cheek. "And now, I've got something for you." He pulled the cycle model from the box and handed it to her.

Dody's face broke into an instant glorious grin. "It's just like your cycle, Spike!"

"It's the exact replica, Punkin."

Laying Katrina carefully aside, she pressed the model lovingly to her. "I like it! I really like it!" she bandied her head about excitedly, her short rust-colored braids flying. "Thank you, Spike."

"You're welcome. And I'm really glad you like it."

Spike lifted her up into his lap and proceeded to explain the various parts to her as the doorbell chimed once more. Sandy crowded in next to them on the divan for the cycle lecture.

Karen hurried to the door feeling happier and more worry-free than she had for months. She swung the door open feeling her smile fade as she looked up into Marc Rodger's deep blue eyes. A shock of lustrous black hair hung charmingly over his forehead.

"Hi, babe," he said greeting her casually.

Karen stood there for a moment too shocked to respond. "I . . . I . . . thought you . . ."

"I'm just about ready to depart the great metropolis of Riverview. They're starting the University summer session in about a week. New challenges and conquests and all of that you understand." He cocked his head to one side arrogantly. "I just wanted to stop by and say, goodbye."

Karen failed to respond to his levity and nonchalance. As far as she was concerned Marc Rodgers had a lot of growing up to do.

"Before you go, I would like you to come in and say goodbye to everyone."

He shook his head. "Hey, babe, I haven't got time for small talk."

He tossed his head back arrogantly. "All right, why not. I've got the Maroon Bomb out front idling. You can't hold it down for too long. It's as excited as I am for the experiences ahead."

"Thanks." Karen backed away from the doorway to allow him to enter.

As they walked across the living room threshold his eyes hurriedly swooped over the occupants. A frown came to his face. "Well, well, all of my favorite people," he said jauntily.

Spike looked up. The hand lying on Dody's knee spontaneously doubled into a fist.

"Spike, Sandy, and Dody, Marc stopped by to say goodbye. He's on his way to the University."

Spike and Sandy sat there without comment.

Dody lurched from Spike's lap and raced to him. She flung herself about his waist embracing him. He stood there rigid completely baffled as to what to do.

"Hey, kid, take it easy." Slowly he pulled himself from her grasp. An embarrassed flush had invaded his face. "I see the Three Musketeers are together once again." He sighed, raising his hands to the ceiling. "I'll never understand. . ."

"I know you never will," Karen said, interrupting.

Marc cocked an eyebrow in a perplexed expression. "Hey, I've got to go." He looked around and tossed his head as he looked over to her.

For just an instant Karen thought she detected a hint of hurt, a hint of regret and then it disappeared. He shrugged and turned toward the door. Dody smiled and waved goodbye to him. He didn't see the gesture. Spike and Sandy looked to one another and shrugged.

Karen walked Marc to the door. He turned at the threshold and looked down upon her.

"Well, I guess this is it."

Karen nodded. "Yes, I guess it is."

Suddenly, he reached out and took her hand.

"We did have some really wonderful times, Marc. That one day in the mountains will always be unforgettable." She looked down to the floor.

"We could have some more good times when I come home on vacations, you know, if you'd only give up that guy."

Karen shook her head slowly. "No, Marc, I don't think so. I don't think our relationship would ever work out. There are too many obstacles."

"You sure?"

"Yes, I'm very sure."

He shrugged. "Well, that's the way it goes I guess. I will say that there was one thing I learned here in Riverview, however."

"Really?" Karen asked curiously. "What was that?"

"Well, I learned that if you want something badly enough you've got to give it all that you've got."

Karen wrinkled her brow in puzzlement. "I don't think I understand."

"I'm talking about track. At least my experience here has convinced me that I've got to be a whole lot more dedicated to track if I'm going to make and stay on a college team."

"Oh," Karen said weakly.

Marc jammed his hands into his pockets and looked out toward the maroon Camaro rumbling at the curb. "Well, I'd better split. It's getting late."

She looked up and smiled. She was glad that the cockiness had faded somewhat. She didn't want to remember him that way.

"I've got just one thing left to do before I go." He quickly leaned forward and kissed her on the lips. Abruptly, before she could say anything, he turned and ran down the sidewalk toward his car.

Karen stood there for several moments her fingertips lightly pressing her lips. Slowly, she turned and walked back into the living room.

Spike and Sandy looked up with concern. Dody stood there with a fixed, puzzled expression.

"You okay?" Spike asked.

"Anything we can do, Karen?" Sandy asked pushing her glasses back up on her nose.

Karen pushed the curtain back from the window and watched the powerful maroon vehicle bolt from the curb and speed down the street. At last, she turned and smiled. "Yes, I'm okay. Now, I'm really okay."

Spike, Sandy, and Dody rushed to her shouting, encircling her in a warm embrace.